Blind Fury

Mark Stephen O'Neal

This is a work of fiction that contains imaginary names, characters, places, events, and incidents not intended to resemble any actual persons, alive or dead, places, events, or incidents. Any resemblances to people, places, events, or incidents are entirely coincidental.

1

Somehow, I found myself sweating in 45-degree weather on a typical Friday afternoon in March of 2012. Each step sent a shockwave up and down my left leg as I tried my very best to get to this job fair before it ended. I had parked for free a mile away from the heart of the Chicago Loop in order to save money, instead of parking inside the thirty-dollar lot across the street from the fair. It was scheduled to be over at two o'clock, so I had given myself an hour and a half to see what options were being offered to me and probably hundreds of other applicants. My name is Julian Brown, and I was laid off from my job six months ago. I've filled out dozens of online applications, but the fact of the matter is that no one was dying to hire a middle-aged accountant, who commands a salary comparable to an eighteen-year vet in the industry.

The pain in my left knee was almost unbearable, and I struggled to cross each intersection before the light changed. I had tweaked my knee while working out a month ago, and it had gotten worse instead of better. I was going to give it one more week before I made an appointment with my doctor because I feared that I might have torn something. I had gained about fifty pounds over the years, and before I had my setback, I was determined to get off the excess weight.

I was two blocks away from the job fair as an elderly woman seemingly zoomed past me while crossing the street at Wacker Drive and State Street. I pulled out a paper towel that I luckily had inside my coat pocket and wiped my face once I arrived safely on the south side of Wacker Drive after nearly being struck by a taxi, and I found myself standing in front of the Wit Hotel, completely winded, moments later. I walked inside the lobby, and security directed me to the staircase. Damn, my knee was in no shape to hike a flight of stairs, I thought.

The recruiters were waiting for me once I finally lumbered up the stairs. A metrosexual looking black guy and an attractive young white woman greeted me in front of a podium, and another Asian young man was on a computer at a desk next to the podium. Numerous millennials were filling out applications to the right of the welcoming committee.

"Hello, sir, what job are you applying for?" the metrosexual guy asked.

"I wanted to apply for the accounting position you had posted," I answered.

"I'm sorry, but that position has been filled," he said, "but you're welcome to apply for the other positions available."

"Okay, thanks," I said.

He handed me an application, and I asked him where the bathroom was. He directed me to walk around the corner to find the bathroom, which was to the left of the young men and women filling out applications. I relieved my bladder, washed my hands, and checked myself in the mirror. I made sure my skin and hair were still intact, and I realized my goatee had more gray in it than I previously noticed.

"Damn, I'm the old man at the club," I said out loud.

And I was the old man at the club indeed because almost everyone outside that bathroom appeared to be under thirty. I never felt so out of place in all my life.

I went back to the application area and found a seat next to a guy who looked closer to my age, and I felt more at ease. I then scanned the application and the sheet with a list of available positions. Nothing remotely peaked my interest because none of the jobs paid even a third of my previous salary. However, I was beginning to feel a sense of desperation because my severance package was almost gone, and unemployment alone didn't come close to covering my monthly expenses. I also didn't plan on dipping into my 401K fund or savings account, but if something didn't open up soon, I would have no choice. I had decided to apply for a mailroom position, even though I had no prior experience.

"Thank you, Mr. Brown," the metrosexual guy said. "We may contact you for an interview after we carefully review your application. Good luck."

"Thank you for your time and consideration," I said.

I left the hotel and flagged down a cab. There was no way in hell I was going to walk back to my car with my knee throbbing and swollen.

"Take me to the corner of Kinzie and Desplaines," I told the cab driver.

"Sure, no problem," he said.

I used to work in the Apparel Center of the Merchandise Mart on the fifth floor, and I was a senior accountant at a mid-level company for almost twenty years. It was the one and only job that I had held since graduating cum laude from Bradley University in the mid-nineties, and with my fortieth birthday quickly approaching, I received a pink slip for an early birthday present. I did everything right professionally—or so I thought—but loyalty didn't carry a whole lot of weight with my former employer. It was easier for them to hire someone half my age and pay them half my salary as opposed to keeping me on the payroll.

"That'll be eleven dollars and ten cents, sir," the cab driver said.

I handed him fifteen dollars and told him to keep the change. My car was parked a little farther down in a secluded spot, but I had the driver let me out at the corner, so I could get a cold Pepsi at Jewels.

I somehow managed to limp for a block to my car across the street from the store only to find my driver side window completely busted and my radio and CDs gone. A thirty-dollar parking lot expense I avoided paying just multiplied tenfold.

2

I was on my way to an auto body shop off 74th and Stony Island that my cut-rate insurance company had assigned to me, and I was still fuming the entire ride there about my window getting busted and my radio getting stolen. I owned a 2003 Hyundai Sonata, so I didn't understand why my car was picked out of the slew of flashier cars parked around mine. I couldn't believe people were still stealing car stereos—I concluded it was probably some vagrant in need of a hit or a fifth of something. Nevertheless, I didn't have the luxury of focusing on it for too long because I had to pick up my son for the weekend after I put my car in the shop and got a rental that the insurance company was going to cover.

My son's name is Miles, and in my mind, he was going to be the next Michael Jordan. I had to admit that I may have lived vicariously through him because of the fact I fell a little short as an athlete growing up. I was a double letterman in high school for football and baseball, but I didn't play organized sports beyond that. Miles was only thirteen and already six feet tall—and he must have gotten his height from my ex-wife Vanessa Stone's side of the family because nobody in my immediate family was over five foot ten. I watched him get his first dunk on a fastbreak in an AAU game a few weeks ago, and college scouts were already looking at him, in addition to the recruiters from various high schools throughout the city.

As luck would have it, the city was doing road construction at the busiest time of the day and on one of the busiest days of the week. Traffic was at a near standstill due to the two right lanes being blocked off from 67th to 71st Street on Stony Island Avenue. I had given up the notion of making it to Vanessa's house in Riverdale by five, so I waited patiently while sipping on the ice-cold Pepsi I bought earlier. A sexy young woman wearing tightfitting stretch denim pants was sashaying across the 67th and Stony Island intersection, and she had my full attention until the light turned green. My hormones were raging because I hadn't been with a woman in over a year, and I hadn't been in a serious relationship since I had split with Vanessa two years ago.

The person behind me honked, and I snapped out of my momentary trance and slowly crossed the intersection. There were still a few yards before the street became one lane, and thankfully, I was already on the far-left lane. Then, in the blink of an eye, a white Cadillac Escalade cut me off and almost hit my car. I didn't see him until it was almost too late, and his music was so loud that I could barely hear him shouting obscenities at me. The guy had let off some combinations that would've made Richard Pryor proud, but I somehow managed to keep my temper in check.

I didn't move my car forward or fire back my own verbal assault at him—I simply looked at him with a blank expression, studying every detail of his face—memorizing the creases on his forehead, the color of his eyes, and the shape of his head and filing it away in my mental Rolodex. This guy had sized me up and labeled me a patsy in a millisecond, and I let him get away with it for the moment. I had reached my boiling point with all the street violence in Chicago long ago, but I wasn't about to stoop to this guy's level and put myself in a potentially dangerous situation. I planned on getting even at a later date, so I also memorized the guy's license plate number.

There was gridlock up to 71st Street, and I could've walked up to the driver's side of his truck and shot him in the head if I chose to do so. However, I had to let it slide because I forgot the .380 semi-auto that I ordinarily kept in my glove compartment. That guy was extremely lucky that I had a memory lapse—who knows what would've transpired if I was strapped that day. Call it divine intervention because my paranoia might've sparked a confrontation worthy of the six o'clock news.

3

The proverbial hole that I fell in got a little deeper as the estimated damage to my car was well over the standard five-hundred-dollar deductible. I was beyond being angry about it at that point, but I tried my best to remain as calm as I possibly could. The two bright spots to this mess were that I got a complimentary ride to the Enterprise Rent-A-Car that was two miles away, and my insurance company covered the rental car expense for thirty days. Thank God for that.

A 2012 Ford Fusion was the ride I picked to be the flavor of the month, and I was out of there in a flash after filling out the necessary paperwork. I arrived at Vanessa's twenty minutes later only to find out Miles was outside playing basketball.

"I told him I was coming at five," I said. "Why isn't he here?"

"You know your son," Vanessa answered. "He eats and sleeps basketball all day, every day."

"Where is he...the park?"

"Yeah, he went there right after school. He didn't waste any time taking advantage of the first day above freezing we've had this month."

"He's just like me. We played ball in the rain, sleet, and snow."

Vanessa paused and said, "Did you buy a new car?"

"Nah, it's a rental. Can you believe some fool busted my window and took my stereo?"

"No...where?"

"Downtown of all places. I parked near the Mart, trying to save a buck for this job fair, and it still ended up costing me a five-hundred-dollar deductible."

"Serves you right...stop being so damn cheap, Julian."

"Yeah, you're right, but did you forget the fact that I don't have a job?"

"But trying to save thirty dollars by avoiding the parking lot just cost you five hundred..."

"I know, and I've already beat myself up enough about it."

"Don't worry. I'll give you the money if things are a little tight for you right now."

"Nah, don't worry about it...I'll be all right."

"Okay."

I looked to the right of the television in the living room and saw Miles's suitcase on the floor.

"I'm going to grab Miles's bag and put it in the trunk. I'll be right back."

Vanessa and I met in college the first day of freshman orientation. She was a breath of fresh air—a five-foot-nine-inch beauty with legs for days and an hourglass figure. Her shoulder-length hair was jet-black and silky, her light brown complexion was flawless, and her smile could brighten any cloudy day. I was hooked the first time I saw her, but it wasn't love at first sight for her. I would soon learn that she liked her men tall and dark chocolate, and unfortunately, I possessed neither of those attributes. We started as friends, and she had cried on my shoulder many nights over a Q-Dog named Bryce Newton, who attended Illinois State University some forty miles away. He was that tall glass of cafe mocha that had her completely strung out our freshman and sophomore year. It turned out that he was seeing her and seeing another girl, who went to Illinois State, at the same time. I was the lucky guy who comforted her and helped her heal her broken heart, and we fell deeply in love afterwards.

We dated our remaining two years at Bradley and got married right after graduation, and most of the sixteen years of marriage were great. We both had great jobs—she was an elementary school teacher, and I, of course, was an accountant. We vacationed in exotic places like the

Cayman Islands or Fuji every summer, and we went to all the Chicago Bulls home games. We had Miles in our fifth year of marital bliss, and things couldn't have been sweeter.

However, things began to take a turn for the worse after the thirteenth year, and we held on for an additional three years before throwing in the towel. I don't really know how we got to that dark place, and I had racked my brain countless times trying to understand why it happened. Maybe the stress of our demanding careers got in the way of our relationship, or maybe the task of raising Miles took a toll on us. All I know is, somewhere down the line, we just stopped communicating with each other.

The divorce was amicable, and we had joint custody of our son. We started as friends and remained friends because of the love and mutual respect we had for one another.

I stepped back inside, and the smell of fried chicken slapped me in the face. Vanessa was always a great cook, in addition to being the most beautiful woman on the planet.

"I'm back," I said. "You mind if I watch TV while I wait?"

"Boy, don't be silly," she answered. "Want something to eat?"

"Nah, I'll pass. It smells good, though."

"You're on a diet again?"

"Yeah, and I'm going to stick to it this time. I started working out last month, but I hurt my knee."

"You better slow down before you have a heart attack."

"I'll keep that in mind."

There was momentary silence, and then I asked, "Why did you really leave me?"

"Huh?"

"I said, I want to know the real reason you left me..."

"Come on, Julian, we've been through this already."

"I know, but I want the truth this time...not some politically correct answer to spare my feelings."

She paused, took a deep breath, and said, "The truth is we were living a lie."

"Living a lie? I was head-over-heels in love with you, Vanessa, and I still get butterflies whenever I see you."

"That's just it...I don't get butterflies whenever I see you anymore, and honestly, I barely remember having them when we were together."

"I don't understand...I thought we were happy, and we had fifteen great years together..."

"Yes, baby, we did. I adored you, but for me, there was something missing that I couldn't put a finger on during the last three or so years of our marriage. As hard as I tried, I couldn't rekindle that spark that we used to have. Eventually, I just couldn't tough it out anymore—not even for Miles. It was better to end the relationship, instead of me cheating on you."

"Did you ever cheat on me?" I asked, my eyes widening and creases forming on my forehead.

"No, Julian, of course not...I would never betray you in any way. Guys would hit on me all the time, but I never entertained any of it."

"You really expect me to believe that? You wouldn't even let me touch you for the last year that we were together."

"I swear I didn't cheat on you, Julian..."

"Then what is it, Vanessa? Was I that bad of a lover?"

"No, baby, you were great...you were always attentive to my needs, and you caressed me in a way that no other man ever had."

"Now, I'm really confused..."

"Don't be...I'm a very complicated woman. There's a side of me that I've never shared with you."

"Oh, yeah? And what side is that?"

"I experimented with women in college, Julian."

"So, you were bisexual?"

"No, not exactly..."

"How many women?"

"Two."

"How come you never told me?"

"I didn't think you'd understand, and I knew you wouldn't have been down with trying a threesome."

"You're damn right I wouldn't have been down with that. You could've at least told me the truth, though."

"I know, and I'm sorry," she said as she stepped back from me.

"Was Bryce into threesomes?"

"Yes, he was. The only two threesomes I ever had were with Bryce, and I never saw those girls again after that."

"Man, this is crazy..."

"I knew you wouldn't understand."

"So, I guess being with me bored you to death..."

"There you go taking everything to the extreme...and no, things weren't boring with you. You made things so much easier for me. You always made me feel comfortable whenever I was with you."

"Isn't that what a mate is supposed to do...make things easier?"

"Yes, Julian, but somewhere down the line, it wasn't enough..."

"What about the girl at I-State?"

"What about her?"

"Did you and Bryce ever have a threesome with her?"

"No, Bryce never told me about her, and that's why we broke up."

"You never knew about each other?"

"No."

"So, if Bryce hadn't cheated on you with the girl at I-State, would you have still been with him?"

"I don't know...maybe."

"You ever see Bryce or talk to him again?"

"No, but I heard he had enough kids to start a tribe by multiple women from several different people I know."

There was an uneasy silence for a couple of minutes, and then she finally said, "I know this may sound like a cliché, but the ending of our marriage was my fault, not yours. You were the perfect husband, and I loved you very deeply. However, I felt empty toward the end of it."

"You felt empty?"

"I don't know, Julian, yes. You asked me why we broke up, and I'm trying to the best of my ability to give you an answer."

"I'm sorry, Vanessa. I didn't mean to upset you."

"It's okay...I'm not upset."

"Well, things weren't all bad...you did give me a beautiful son."

"Yes, I did, didn't I?"

We gave each other a warm embrace after there was nothing else left to say, and I kissed her on the cheek. She wiped a tear from her eye, and I wiped away a tear of my own. A part of me felt like she betrayed me, but not because she did things with Bryce that she would never do with me. I felt betrayed because she wasn't totally honest about the person she truly was, and my already bruised ego took yet another hit.

"I'm going to take off," I said. "I'll pick up Miles at the park and have him back Sunday evening."

"That's fine. See you on Sunday."

"Okay, see you Sunday."

4

I left Vanessa's and drove around the block to Ivanhoe Park, which was right by the Metra train station. There were police and an ambulance blocking off the street when I arrived, and I suddenly felt a cold sensation throughout my body. Then I parked my car and rushed over to the scene to find out what was going on. My heart dropped to the ground when I saw Miles on a gurney with his shirt drenched in blood and an oxygen mask over his face.

"What happened to my son?!" I asked one of the paramedics tersely.

"Sir, step back and let us do our job," one of the paramedics said.

"Who did this to my son?!" I shouted to the top of my lungs.

One of the policemen tried to restrain me and shouted, "Step back and let the paramedics do their job, sir!"

"What the hell happened here?" I asked.

"There were shots fired, and unfortunately, your son got caught in the crossfire," the policeman answered.

"Did you catch the guy who did this?" I asked. "Why was someone shooting at him? He's a good kid..."

"We don't believe he was the intended target, sir," the policeman answered. "I promise you that we will get to the bottom of this..."

The ambulance was motioning to pull off, and I walked toward the driver's side of the ambulance.

"That's my son you have back there," I said to the paramedics. "Can I ride with him?"

"Okay, sir," one of the paramedics answered. "You can ride on the passenger side."

"Thank you," I said. "Where are you taking him?"

"To Christ Advocate Hospital."

I sat down inside the ambulance and promptly called Vanessa.

"Meet me at Christ Hospital as soon as possible," I urged her.

"What happened, Julian?" she asked.

"Miles got shot, and it doesn't look good..."

"Oh my God! Where are you?!"

"We're on our way the hospital..."

"Alright, I'll meet you there."

I disconnected the call, and the ambulance pulled off. Vanessa's entire family was at the hospital when we arrived at the emergency entrance. Her parents and her younger sister, Geneva, lived in Evergreen Park, which is a hop, skip, and a jump from Christ Advocate Hospital in Oak Lawn. Geneva was crying, and her parents had a look of utmost concern. I also called my brother, Jake, and told him to meet me there, but he lived on the other side of town near the 55th Street beach off Lake Shore Drive. Jake and I were originally from St. Louis, so I opted not to tell our parents yet. I was going to give them a call as soon as I had some definitive news to tell them.

We stood by the hospital waiting room patiently, and Jake and Vanessa finally arrived. Vanessa looked me in the eyes and asked, "How did this happen, Julian?"

"I think it was a drive-by shooting," I answered. "The police don't know anything yet."

"It's a damn shame, Julian," my father-in-law said. "No place is safe anymore."

"How is he?" Jake asked.

"He's stable as far as we know, but the doctor hasn't told us anything new," I answered.

"We should bow our heads in prayer," my mother-in-law said.

She led us in prayer for several minutes, and the doctor came out shortly afterwards to give us an update.

"How is my son?" I asked the doctor. "Is he conscious?"

"He's lost a lot of blood, but we were able to stabilize him by giving him a blood transfusion," the doctor answered. "He's still in intensive care, and we have to operate in order to remove the bullet from his chest."

"How soon are you going to operate on him?" Vanessa asked.

"We're going to start the surgery immediately, ma'am," the doctor answered. "The good news is that he's AB positive."

"What does that mean?" Vanessa asked.

"It means he can receive blood from anyone," the doctor answered.

"Thank you, doctor," I said.

The doctor nodded and went back to my son's room to prep him for surgery. We all sat back down in our seats in silence and waited in anguish for what seemed like a lifetime. Geneva seemed to be taking it harder than anybody else, so I sat down next to her on the sofa and tried to comfort her as best as I could.

"You all right, little sis?" I asked.

"Yeah, I'm okay," she answered.

"Want me to get you a cup of coffee?"

"No, thank you, Julian."

"Miles is a fighter, you know...he's gonna pull through this."

"Yes, I know. My nephew's gonna pull through, and this whole nightmare is gonna be over."

I kissed her on the cheek and got up from the sofa. I decided to walk outside to get some fresh air. The mood was just too somber for me to stomach at that moment, and I didn't want to shed tears in front of everyone.

Geneva had been having a hard time personally, and she had just about reached her breaking point after Miles got shot. She graduated from Illinois State University with a finance degree five years ago, but with the economy being the way it was, she hadn't been able to find gainful employment yet.

I was having a hard time myself, and I felt like the walls were beginning to close in on me. I tried to focus on something simple and pleasant, like the smell of Vanessa's fried chicken or one of our trips to Fiji, to no avail because all I could do was think about Miles. He had everything going for him—he was smart, athletic, and very handsome.

He was going to be successful no matter what he chose to do with his life, and now, all of that was in jeopardy.

I finally mustered up the strength to go back to the waiting area a half hour or so later, and the doctor was talking to the family when I stepped inside the room. The grim look on his face said it all—and Vanessa nearly collapsed onto the floor before Jake had to hold her up, my father-in-law tried to comfort my mother-in-law, and Geneva broke down crying. I stepped toward Geneva and embraced her tightly, while trying with all my might to keep my own sanity. No words could describe the pain I was in, once I learned Miles died from internal hemorrhaging, and all the hopes and dreams that we had for him were swallowed up like a deadly tsunami devouring an entire Indonesian town without warning.

5

Three Months Later....

There was a sink full of dirty dishes and a month's worth of dirty laundry that needed my full attention, but I hadn't had the desire to do much of anything except find out who killed Miles. The police had no new leads in the weeks following his funeral, and ultimately, my son's murder became a cold case.

I couldn't just sit around idly and waste away, physically and mentally. I tried to channel my negative emotions toward being as positive as I possibly could, but I was losing that battle with each passing day. My anger roared like a raging inferno, and the only two things that kept me sane were my strenuous workouts and extreme wind downs with Jack Daniels. I woke up fuming every single day, and I would run on my treadmill or lift weights until my muscles ached in order to release my anger. When exercising didn't work, I would down almost a fifth of whiskey every day to try to numb the pain.

I pounded the pavement in search of answers whenever I wasn't trying to kill myself, but I hadn't gotten anywhere with my efforts. I had knocked on the neighbors' doors across the street from the park in order to find out if anyone saw what happened, and I questioned some of Miles's friends. Unfortunately, nobody had a clue about why Miles got shot. I printed flyers and offered a $10,000 chunk out of my 401K as a reward for anyone who knew who my son's killer was.

The only thing I did find out by keeping my ear to the streets was that Miles wasn't the intended target. He was simply at the wrong place at the wrong time when two rival gang factions were banging it out over turf, and their beef erupted on the basketball court. I felt that the punk who shot Miles would eventually run his mouth and brag about what he had done to somebody. I planned on seizing the opportunity to overhear that conversation by frequenting every bar in the area for the last few months. The streets were always talking, but in order to be able to hear what the streets were saying, you had to be in the right place at the right time. Sooner or later, I was going to hit pay dirt.

My doorbell rang, and I slowly got up from the couch. My head was still throbbing from the half-bottle of whiskey I consumed with reckless abandon the previous night. I looked through the peephole and saw it was Jake.

"What's up, Julian?" he asked. "I thought you fell off the face of the earth."

"That was the plan," I answered. "I'm hoping I'll wake up one day and be gone from this godforsaken hell hole."

"You don't mean that..."

"I'm dead serious, Jake. I pray that you don't ever lose any of your girls because I wouldn't wish this pain on anybody."

"I wish I could tell you that things will get better, but I'd be lying to you if I did."

"You don't have to say anything because I already know things won't get better. This hole in my heart is here to stay."

"What you got planned today?" Jake asked, changing the subject.

"What the hell does it look like?" I asked rhetorically.

"Come on, Julian. It's a beautiful Saturday morning. Let's go out for breakfast...my treat, okay?"

"Nah, I'm good. I don't feel like going anywhere today."

"You know, you look like you've been dealing with your issues fairly well...I mean...you look like you're in great shape, physically, at least."

"Yeah, I've lost a lot of weight, but truthfully, I'm not doing too well."

"You wanna talk about it?"

"No, I don't think talking is going to do any good. I'm not suicidal, but I'm afraid that, if somebody so much as look at me the wrong way, all hell is going to break loose."

"All the more reason to talk about it."

"Really? And what good is talking about it going to do? Nothing is going to bring Miles back."

"I know, and I'm very sorry about that. I loved Miles, too."

"I know you did. I don't mean to snap on you..."

"It's okay, little brother. That's what I'm here for."

"Thanks for stopping by."

"You're my brother...I had to make sure you are all right."

"I'll live."

"Oh, by the way, I ran that plate you gave me."

"Yeah? What did you find out?"

"That guy was bad news. He had a rap sheet longer than both our arms."

"Did you pick him up?"

"Yeah, we had a traffic warrant out on him, and he was a suspect in a robbery."

"Wow, no surprise there."

Jake paused and said, "Good work, though. I told you I can get you on if you don't let your fortieth birthday pass."

"Like I said before, I'm no cop."

"Whatever you say. I'll see you later."

"Take care, Jake."

We gave each other a hug, and he left. Saturdays were usually Jake's busiest, most crime-ridden days after he was promoted to detective ten years ago, but I guess he took the day off to be with me. I felt bad about blowing him off, but the truth was, I still didn't want to be bothered with anybody. He was the first person from the family to see me face-to-face since the funeral.

I had completely cut myself off from everyone, and I hadn't taken any calls in the last month. Vanessa had called me every day for two weeks, but eventually, her phone calls stopped. She probably felt I abandoned her, and in a sense, I did. Miles was the bond that kept us together, and now that he was gone, I felt there was no need to continue our relationship. To me, it was much easier that way.

I plopped back down on the couch and got back under my blanket. An empty fifth of Jack Daniels stared back at me, and I realized my head was still throbbing. I wasn't ready to face the world yet, so I took some Tylenol and went back to sleep.

6

I awakened to the sound of my doorbell, and I looked out my window and saw the sun was beginning to set. I had slept the whole day for the umpteenth time, and I instantly felt grumpy when I noticed again that I was out of whiskey. The doorbell rang again, and I slowly got up to answer it.

"What do you want, Vanessa?" I asked angrily, while looking out of the peephole. "I don't feel like being bothered."

"Open the damn door," she demanded. "I'm not taking no for an answer."

I opened the door shirtless with a pair of Nike shorts on and asked, "What?"

She looked taken aback when I opened the door, and she rubbed on my much smaller stomach and said, "You're looking well in spite of the circumstances."

"Looks can be deceiving. So, what brings you by?"

"You won't take any of my calls. What was I supposed to do?"

"Respect my damn privacy and go on with your life."

"So, what are you gonna do, sleep your life away?"

"Yeah, that's exactly what I plan on doing."

"So, you're just gonna give up, huh? I loved Miles just as much as you did, but you don't see me giving up."

"Maybe you should...if we were such good parents, he'd still be here."

"Nope, nope, nope...I'm not gonna let you dump on me or yourself. What happened to our son could've happened to anybody."

"Why do you care, anyway? We don't have ties to each other anymore, now that our son is dead."

"Is that what you think? You're just gonna cut me out of your life? I thought we were better than that."

"Don't act like there's something more than what it is...you left me, remember?"

"I miss my friend, Julian..."

"Friendship is overrated, and besides, you couldn't even keep it real with me."

"Wow. You're still on that? I knew you couldn't handle the truth."

"I don't like being played like a fool..."

"I didn't play you, Julian."

"It's okay...really. I was indeed your doormat, but those days are long gone."

"So, it's all or nothing with you, huh?"

"No, there is no 'all or nothing' to this equation, Vanessa. The Julian you once knew died on that operating table with Miles."

"Look, Julian, I know you're hurting, and I know the void of losing Miles will never go away. You aren't the only one who can't sleep or eat, you know, and you're the only other person who knows exactly what I'm going through."

"Yes, Vanessa, I know exactly what you're going through. But seeing you reminds me of Miles, and that's way too painful for me."

"We can help each other get through the pain...we're still family, like it or not."

I raised my right index finger in protest and was about to retort, but I had no words. I knew it was wrong to cut off her and everybody close to me, so I stood quietly for a brief moment.

I finally broke the silence and said, "You're right, we are family. Just give me some time, all right?"

"I can respect that," she said. "Make sure you call me later."

"Okay, we can do lunch or something in a few days."

"I'm gonna hold you to that..."

I gave her hug and basically told her what she wanted to hear in order to get her out of my house. Whew. However, seeing Jake and Vanessa did lift my spirits somewhat, and I finally mustered up enough energy to pick myself up off the couch and take a shower. Surprisingly, I wasn't filled with uncontrollable rage at the end of the day for a change. I decided to head out and have a drink at a bar around the corner from my house in Chatham, a relatively quiet neighborhood on the south side of town.

The NBA Finals game was on when I stepped inside the bar, so I grabbed a seat directly in front of the television screen. There were only a few patrons inside, but one in particular caught my eye. She was unequivocally gorgeous—her five-foot-seven-inch frame possessed curves in all the right places, and she oozed an enormous amount of sex appeal.

Her black weave with blonde streaks complimented her smooth, buttermilk complexion; her black mini-dress accentuated her shapely derriere, hips, and thighs, and her black stiletto ankle boots made her calves explode. Her right thigh had tattoos of small, hollow stars that looked like a winding road from the middle of her thigh to the top of her leg; she also had a tattoo of a heart with an arrow going through it right above her right breast. Trouble. She sported a black and gray Michael Kors purse with a gold MK emblem on it that matched her entire outfit. The most captivating feature of all was her big, piercing brown eyes because they seemed to see right through me, giving me a glimpse of how dangerously seductive she could be. She gave me the impression that she could go from zero to one hundred in a millisecond if provoked.

Even though she was by far one of the most captivating women I'd ever laid eyes on, she looked relatively young—maybe twenty-five or twenty-six—but definitely no older than thirty. I was about to see how rusty my game was after I paid the bartender for my Miller Draft. She was standing alone by the jukebox.

"I like that new song by Drake," I said, trying to appear as though I was up on the new music. "Do they have it yet?"

She turned around to face me with an emotionless expression and said nothing. I knew, at that moment, she thought I was lame, but I didn't care. I still had supreme confidence in myself after hooking Vanessa almost twenty years ago, so some twenty-five-year-old millennial wasn't about to damage my ego too much.

"We don't have to listen to Drake," I added, trying to break the ice. "Two Chains is cool, too."

"You can listen to whatever the hell you want when you put your own money in," she said in a sassy tone.

"You're absolutely right, beautiful. I'm Julian, by the way. Can I buy you a drink?"

"No, thank you."

"Well, can I talk to you then? I'm just trying to get to know you, baby."

"I'm not your baby, and like Drake said on his song, *I don't need no new friends.*"

"Alrighty, then...sorry I bothered you."

I walked back to the bar with my tail between my legs, and even with my fresh gear on and clean-shaven face, I was *still* the old man at the club. I then gulped the last of my beer and ordered another one with a whiskey shot. My goal was to get as wasted as I could in the shortest amount of time possible and stumble home. Little did I know that my life was about to change forever, drastically.

7

It was an hour or so later, and I was buzzed out of my mind. I consumed shot after shot without monitoring my binging, and the guy who appeared to be fresh out of Bartending School didn't stop me from drinking myself into oblivion. The room was starting to spin around me, and the haze of my intoxication rendered me almost immobile in my seat.

I looked to my right and noticed the girl from the jukebox staring in my direction while talking to some guy. The dude was mean-mugging me, and he had two other guys following suit. Moments later, the group walked toward me with bad intentions. I acted as though I didn't see either one of them as I continued to down my drink.

"So, this is the chump that tried to talk to my girl," the ringleader said.

He sort of looked like the rapper Young Buck, and I was so drunk that I almost asked him for an autograph but refrained from being a sarcastic prick. I turned to my right to make eye contact with him.

"No disrespect, homeboy," I said, "but I didn't know she was your girl."

"You better watch yourself before you get yourself caught up," he said forcefully. "Make this the last time I see you in here, understand?"

I quickly learned that trying to reason with him was a colossal waste of time. My goal at that point was to get out of the bar unscathed but not without a few choice words.

"The last time I checked, we all live in a free society," I said as I began to sober up somewhat quickly. "You need to raise up off me before you catch a bad break."

"From who, you?" he asked. "Man, you better make yourself scarce before you end up in a body bag, homie!"

I downed the last of my drink and said, "Because I'm a peaceful brother, I'm gonna give you what you want...this time. Y'all be cool."

"This ain't over," he said.

I put my glass on the bar and walked out. I could feel the heat of their stares on my back as I checked my waist for the two semi-autos I had tucked underneath my leather jacket secured in their holsters. I bought the second one a couple of weeks after Miles got killed, and I never left home without them after what happened to him. Law or no law, I refused to be a sitting duck while the criminals roamed freely with heat tucked in their pants and used the rest of us as target practice.

I can't believe that girl kicked the whole thing off just because I stepped to her. I didn't think I was disrespectful or offensive, but I guess it wasn't up to me to decide what was offensive to her. Damn, though, she had to know she was going to get some attention the moment she left the house with that outfit she had on—a mini-skirt that fit her so tightly one could see every curve of her body—and I could clearly see she wasn't wearing any underwear. I sincerely felt it was my duty as a man at least to say hi to her.

I had a sudden urge to urinate and knew I couldn't make it home without having an accident on myself, so I scurried to the alley behind my house to drain my bladder. It was an atypical, briskly cool night in June—maybe in the mid-fifties—and the wind nearly blew my stream onto my pants. Then, without warning, I was surrounded by my nemesis and his flunkies from the bar before I could completely zip up my pants. The girl stood next to her man with her arms folded and a sassy look on her face.

Click, clack.

One of them held a gun in his right hand by his side, and the ringleader pulled back his jacket to reveal that he had his burner tucked inside his pants. I looked him in the eye and smiled.

"Didn't anybody ever tell you that having a smart mouth can get you in trouble, my man?" Young Buck's twin said.

"Man, why do y'all insist on coming at me?" I answered a question with a question.

"You started it by trying to holla at my girl," he stated.

"Maybe if your girl didn't dress like a hooker, nobody would bother her," I said.

"What did you say?" the girl asked tersely.

"I speak very clearly, and I don't like repeating myself," I answered.

"Get ready to die, sucka," Young Buck's twin said. "And after I make Swiss cheese outta you, I'mma take your wallet, that jacket you got on, and them shoes, playa."

"Oh, now I get it," I said. "This whole damn scene is a setup. I have to admit though, y'all have a smooth hustle going on here."

"That's right, and you're gonna be my next score," he said.

"You're such a damn cliché," I said, shaking my head. "Guys are always trying to make a come-up by robbing their own damn people or slinging dope. What's the matter; you can't get your rap career off the ground?"

"That's it, my man," he said. "You've just crossed the line!"

The guy with the Glock in his right hand tried to raise his arm, but I had already drawn my twin .380 semi-autos from their holsters underneath my jacket.

"Bang, bang, bang, bang, bang...."

I caught the four of them off-guard and opened fire on the three men. Flunky number one managed to get off one shot before I shot him in the chest, and I nearly emptied both clips in the ringleader and his other flunky. The girl ran and hid behind a garbage can before I let off my first shot, but I didn't shoot her, even though she was just as responsible. I checked myself to see if I'd been hit and felt nothing.

The three of them lay on the ground exactly like a chalk outline. I looked to see if there were any witnesses or neighbors in the window and didn't notice a thing before I tucked my guns back in their respective holster.

"You are a dead man!" she shouted. "There's nowhere on earth for you to hide from my hitters!"

"I'm not hiding anywhere, missy!" I retorted. "And for the record, this is all your fault! Your friends would still be here if you didn't kick the whole thing off."

I ran down the alley and left the girl on the ground, sobbing and holding her dead boyfriend, after I heard sirens in the distance. I needed to get to my house and pack some clothes before I found an extended-stay motel to lay low for a few weeks. Fortunately, my house was the first on the corner, and I had a side door entrance and didn't have to go around the front.

I quickly packed some clothes and locked up my house. My car was also parked on the side of the house on 82nd Street instead of Michigan Avenue. I then hit the expressway, which was a couple of blocks from my house, in record time.

8

I continued to drive south on Interstate 55 after I fled the crime scene that night and ended up back home in St. Louis. I was exhausted and had come down from the adrenaline rush of shooting and killing three people. I needed to crash because it was almost daybreak, but I didn't go to my parents' house. I booked a room at a Holiday Inn, instead, because I didn't feel like answering a barrage of questions as to why I was in town.

I also wondered how I'd feel after the night that changed my life forever in the days to follow. Guilt? Shame? Indifference? The truth of the matter was, killing them didn't bring me any sort of satisfaction or bring back my son. Knowing that they would never rob or kill again did help me rationalize my actions. Call it murder, call it vigilante justice, call it whatever you want—I felt it was self-defense and would do it again if put in the same situation. If I didn't react the way that I did, the only person dead in that alley would have been me.

Jake tried calling me a couple of days after the shooting, but I ignored his call. Once I finally spoke to him, I told him that I was out of town during that time to clear my head. It wasn't entirely a lie—being in St. Louis proved to be therapeutic, if nothing else.

It was 6:53 am once I hit city limits, so I decided to get something to eat and swing by my cousin, DeQuan Buckner's, house afterward. He lived in the quiet suburb of Berkeley near the Lambert International Airport. He was also an early riser, so I assumed he was up. He attended Bradley University at the same time I did and majored in computer science. Unlike me, he couldn't stomach corporate America for too long, so once he learned everything he needed to know in his field, he started his own internet security business and never looked back.

His car was in the driveway when I pulled up in front of his house, and I parked my car behind his car. He opened the door five seconds after I rang the doorbell and must have seen me drive up from his front window.

"What's up, cuz," DeQuan said as we embraced.

"I can't call it," I answered.

"Once again, I'm sorry about Miles."

"Thanks, man."

"So, what brings you in town?"

"I might have gotten myself in big trouble, Quan."

"Trouble? What kind of trouble, Julian?"

"I shot and killed three people last night. I've been driving all night long with the gun residue still on my fingertips, trying to wrap my mind around what just happened, but I can't get the image of those three dead guys out of my head."

"You shot and killed three people? Have you lost your damn mind?"

"It was self-defense, Quan..."

"Damn, man, I know you're still hurting because of Miles, but what have you gotten yourself into?"

"I was minding my own business at this bar around the corner from my house...well, not exactly minding my business..."

"Look, nobody's blaming you, man...hell, it's a war zone up there. So, what happened?"

"It was all because of this chick I tried to step to at the bar, but she was just a plant sent to set up some poor, unsuspecting fool."

"Some poor, unsuspecting fool like you."

"Yeah, exactly like me. And my game was rusty as hell, too. Her guy and two goons were going to rob and shoot me in the damn alley, but I unloaded my two semi-autos on them."

"Did you kill the girl?"

"Nah, man, she wasn't packing any heat."

"You shouldn't have left any witnesses. What if she snitches on you?"

"That's not how I do things, and besides, we never exchanged names."

"That doesn't matter, Julian. I'm sure there's some camera footage of you from the club or from a police camera somewhere."

"Man, those cameras don't half work...and hopefully, she won't tell the police anything."

"I'm sorry that happened to you, Julian," DeQuan said, looking me directly in the eyes, "but we have to get rid of those guns. We can't have the police trace them back to you."

"What are you going to do with them?" I asked, my heartbeat quickening after the reality of the situation began to set in.

"Let me worry about that..."

"I didn't tell you this to get you involved, Quan."

"Too late...I'm already involved."

"Are you going to disassemble them?"

"Yes, disassemble and destroy them. I have an electric saw and blow torch that will do the job, so don't worry, okay?"

"How do you know anything about destroying a gun?"

"I'm a mechanic, carpenter, and a computer geek all rolled up in one, remember? There's nothing I can't build or take apart."

"Right..."

"Do you doubt my skills?"

"No, it's not that. My mind won't stop racing."

"Don't fret over this. You did what you had to do, and I know what you're thinking. God won't condemn you for this..."

"I know—true repentance, but my lifestyle hasn't been anything God-like."

"Man, stop it. Uncle June and Aunt Mavis really did a number on you, cuz," he chuckled. "They had you and Jake in church every Sunday."

"And look where all that Bible studying has gotten me—my wife left me, I lost my job, my son was murdered, and I just killed three people. My life is, in a nutshell, screwed up."

"You still got life, bruh...as long as you are breathing, you have a chance to turn things around. If you need a fresh start, you can come back home and live with me until you get back on your feet."

"I don't know. I'll think about it."

"You might as well come back home because there's nothing really keeping you in Chicago. You know, you and Jake left me here to fend for myself while you all planted roots up there."

"Hey, you could've left St. Louis, too. You just didn't want to leave Gina..."

"Yeah, she was scared to start over in a new city, and she didn't want to quit her job. I stayed here because I didn't want to lose her."

"And for all the good that did. You two split up, just like Vanessa and me."

"Well, at least Vanessa isn't trying to break you with alimony and child support payments. Gina quit her job not long after we got married and hasn't worked since."

"Damn, alimony and child support."

"Don't get me wrong...I love my kids and wouldn't trade them for anything in this world, but if I had it to do all over again, I would've left St. Louis with you and Jake."

"What's done is done, and you can't dwell on that. You and Gina got married because you were meant to be together at that time."

"Yeah, you're right. Jake and Cindy are the last couple standing."

"Yeah, and I need to know what their secret is."

I paused for a moment and said, "I'm tired as hell, man. I booked a room at the Holiday Inn, so I'm about to crash."

"Nope, I ain't having it," DeQuan said. "You're gonna crash here, so cancel your reservation."

"Are you sure? Because I'm not trying to cramp your style..."

"It's cool, cuz. I'm single, and that's not about to change anytime soon. I've got alimony payments for at least another ten years, and if Madison goes to college, tack on four more years. I'm in no hurry to jump into something else right now."

"I totally understand, bro. I was lucky Vanessa waived alimony, and the child support that I pay is more than fair."

"Vanessa's a good woman. I wished you two could've worked things out."

"Me, too, but there's a lot that you don't know about her."

"True, but that's your business, man. Besides, nobody's perfect."

"This is true."

"Anyway, the guest room is yours. Stay as long as you want."

"Thanks, I appreciate this."

"No problem."

I went into the guest room and sat on the bed before taking off my shoes. I didn't remember doing anything else after my face hit the pillow.

9

I anticipated that the police would arrest me in the weeks to follow, but surprisingly, nothing happened. No witnesses came forward, the police had no leads, and the media reported the killings as *gang related*. Wow, the girl from the club didn't snitch—staying true to the game by not breaking the code of the streets. That by no means meant that I was in the clear, and if I was a betting man, I would bet everything in my pocket that she took a snapshot of me at that club and sent my image to her "hitters."

I ended up staying in St. Louis for a week, and then it was back to my painful reality when I finally came home to an empty house. I also saw my parents while I was there, and spending time with them proved to be surprisingly less stressful than I anticipated—only a few questions about my reasons for coming home unannounced. Growing up as a preacher's kid wasn't easy, but it kept me on the straight and narrow path to success. They still lived in the same neighborhood where Jake and I were raised, which was Ferguson, Missouri. They didn't judge my situation like they would have done in years past, and they were just happy that I was back home.

It was going to be a beautiful Saturday night weather-wise, so I decided to get out of the house to celebrate Jake's forty-fifth birthday with him. And his contemporary-looking, four-bedroom condo was the perfect place to throw a party. Most of the people there were his cop friends—which made me slightly uncomfortable, given my present circumstances—and he invited Vanessa. I totally disapproved of that, but it was his party. To him, she was and would always be family.

I copped a seat at his bar with my beer in hand and kept to myself. I was there to support my brother, not to socialize. Jake's wife, Cindy, had an entire spread of food—chicken, roast beef, spaghetti, and potato salad to name a few things—but I didn't have much of an appetite.

In walked this unbelievably sexy woman moments later—five-foot-five with the most beautiful, hypnotizing hazel-brown eyes I had ever seen. She was wearing this zebra-print dress that gripped her buxom body like a leather glove once she removed her jacket, and her eccentric style captivated me from the start. Every inch of her body seemed to have curves—thick in the thighs and derriere, small in the waist and large in the bosom. Her caramel complexion didn't have a trace of acne, pimples, or moles, and her low-cut fade hairstyle was unique. Vanessa walked in behind her, and the two of them made their rounds saying hello to the people Vanessa knew at the party.

I played off my instant attraction to Vanessa's friend by not gawking at her, but the image of her was already tattooed in my brain. Vanessa finally came over where I was sitting and introduced this mystery woman to me.

"Hello, Vanessa," I said as I stood to give her a hug and kiss on the cheek.

"Hey, Julian, I want you to meet my friend, Batavia Lovejoy," Vanessa said.

"Nice to meet you, Julian," Batavia said, extending her hand to me.

"Likewise," I said.

"We're going to grab something to eat," Vanessa said. "Talk to you later."

"Okay," I said.

They walked toward the kitchen while I continued to sip on my brew. Cindy checked on me to see if I needed anything after I'd spent nearly an hour at the bar drinking. She could tell I was preoccupied with my thoughts.

"Are you all right over here?" Cindy asked. "You haven't said more than two words to anybody tonight."

"I'm cool, sis," I answered.

"You want me to wrap your plate to go?" she asked.

"Yes, thanks," I answered. "I don't have much of an appetite right now, but I'm sure I'll be hungry later."

"Good, I wouldn't want you to miss out on this good food. And just so you know, Miles was like a son to me, Julian. I miss him so much."

"Thank you for saying that, Cindy. I know how much he meant to you and Jake."

"If you ever need to talk to someone, don't hesitate to call me, Julian."

"I appreciate that, sis...thank you."

Cindy went to the kitchen to make my plate, and I noticed Vanessa and Batavia sitting on the couch on the opposite side of the room, eating and conversing with each other. The vibe I got from them suggested that they were more than just friends—maybe it was the fact that Vanessa was practically sitting in Batavia's lap, or maybe it was how they smiled at each other and gazed in each other's eyes, or maybe it was because I was the only other person who knew her dirty little secret. Nevertheless, their relationship was none of my business, so I quickly turned my focus away from them.

Moments later, I got up from my chair to look for Jake. I couldn't stomach Vanessa making goo-goo eyes at her date anymore, so I took it as my cue to leave. I found Jake in the kitchen talking to one of his cop friends.

"I'm gonna take off, Jake," I said.

"Leaving us so soon, huh?" he asked.

"Yeah, I'm a little tired, and I've got some yard work to do tomorrow," I answered.

"Well, thanks for coming," he said.

"Wouldn't miss it for the world," I said. "Later."

"Later," he said, giving me some dap and a hug.

I walked back inside to get my coat and said my goodbyes to the rest of the people I knew. Cindy gave me my to-go plate, and I let out a sigh of relief once I stepped out into the hallway and made my way to the elevator. I then pressed the button to go down to the lobby, and I heard someone shout my name.

"Julian!" Vanessa shouted again. "Wait, don't leave yet!"

I turned around and saw Vanessa and Batavia walking toward me. The elevator door chimed and opened, but I let the door close.

"What's up, Vanessa?" I asked.

"Batavia and I are about to go to that new club downtown right off of Wells and Division," she said. "Wanna come with us?"

"Nah, I'm good," I answered. "Thanks for asking, though."

"Aw, come on, Julian. It'll be fun," Batavia said coyly. "I'd love it if you come with us."

"As tempting as you make it sound, Batavia, I will have to pass," I said. "I have a ton of stuff to do tomorrow morning, but I'll take a rain check on hanging out with y'all."

Vanessa pecked Batavia on the lips, and she turned to me and said, "You really don't know what you're missing, baby."

Both of them looked at me seductively after Vanessa's statement, and I felt my nature begin to rise. I considered their offer for a second or two but quickly shot it down in my mind.

"I'm good, ladies," I said, pretending to be naive of what Vanessa was really suggesting. "I'll hang out with the two of you some other time, okay?"

"Okay," Batavia said with a pouting expression.

"We're gonna hold you to that," Vanessa said.

"I'm sure you will."

They turned around and walked hand in hand back to Jake's party. I shook my head and pressed the elevator button to go down again.

10

I was trying to get as close to normalcy as I possibly could, even though my life would never be the same again. I had gone on a few job interviews and finally landed a full-time position as an assistant manager at a local retail store chain. Not exactly what I had in mind, but I had to do something to pay the bills.

The police had no new leads on the triple homicide that practically happened in my backyard, according to Jake, because they were looking for known suspects—guys who were deep in the streets and not forty-year-old ex-accountants like me. I was so far below the radar that I didn't have to worry about them ever sniffing at my door unless the young lady from the club told the police about me. The closest I've ever come to violating the law before that night was racking up a few parking and speeding tickets, and the last speeding ticket I got was on a road trip back to school some twenty years ago. I'd all but put the whole ordeal out of my mind at that point and was just focusing on getting my life back on track. Nobody would ever know what I did because I definitely wasn't going to say anything to anyone.

I had worked the morning shift all week long and decided to have a drink somewhere once I got off this particular night. There were a couple of new joints that I wanted to check out in the south suburbs, so I headed to this spot off Dixie Highway in Harvey called the *Cozy Inn*. It looked like the typical bar once I entered the parking lot and went inside. It was a little after seven, so it was still fairly empty.

The bartender was a pretty lady, who resembled Jade Pickett before she became Pickett-Smith. Same hairstyle from *Jason Lyric* and the sassiness to boot. I asked her for a shot of Jack Daniels and the name of the perfume she was wearing because it smelled so good on her. She frowned, and then she sighed before she told me she was wearing Hanae Mori. I laughed and told her I was thinking of buying that same fragrance for my girlfriend, even though I didn't have one—I was hoping she would be my girlfriend—or at least my girl for the night.

Our conversion lasted all but two minutes, and I could tell she wasn't the slightest bit interested in me. I guessed that she probably got hit on at the very least ten times a night, and my unwanted flirtations were par for the course.

I decided to take my drink and walk around to examine the place. There was a room with a couple of pool tables and a dartboard on the back wall near the pool tables. There were also several vacant rooms with mirrors and leather chairs—undoubtedly reserved for private lap dances because it was a strip club on certain nights. It was a Thursday, so I wasn't sure if the girls were dancing that night. I wasn't really there to make it rain—I wanted to unwind with a drink and some good music.

The club started to fill up a couple of hours later, and a couple of shapely young ladies with gym bags had walked in. That confirmed it was indeed stripper night at the Cozy Inn, and there were more guys than women present for the show.

It suddenly hit me that I had no friends, other than my brother Jake, and I realized I cut everyone else off once Vanessa and I got married. I was all about her and the family we created, and I didn't devote time to maintaining my friendships with guys I had known since high school and college. I would run into some of them from time to time, and those brief encounters would always end with the exchanging of numbers and promises of hooking up at a later date. Unfortunately, neither party kept the promise of keeping in touch.

I recalled having one of the most interesting and bizarre conversations I ever had with DeQuan and two of my college buddies the first semester of our sophomore year while I was sipping on my fifth drink. There were four of us hanging out in my dorm room with a case of Budweiser and a pan of chicken wings one weekend before final exams, and the sun was coming up before we had all passed out from drinking.

"How you think you gonna do this semester, JB?" DeQuan asked me.

"I should get a 4.0, hopefully," I answered. "All I have to do is get no less than B's on all my finals, and I should be good."

"Damn, I'll be lucky to get a 2.0 this semester," Ronnie interjected.

"Man, aren't you already on probation?" DeQuan asked.

"Yeah," Ronnie answered. "Too much partying and skirt chasing, my friend."

"That's messed up," DeQuan said. "Now I'm gonna have to find another roommate if you get booted outta here."

"I'll be all right," Ronnie said. "How did you do, Quan?"

"I did great," DeQuan answered. "Best case scenario...a 4.0."

"What's the worst-case scenario?" I asked.

"If I get a B in Political Science, I'll get a 3.8," DeQuan answered. "I'm a lock to get A's in my other four classes."

I nodded and said, "You're kind of quiet over there, Jason. What are you reading?"

"The Bible," he answered. "I'm looking over the Book of Matthew."

"Man, put the good book down and grab a beer, homie," Ronnie urged. "That can wait until Sunday."

"Are you going to tell Jesus to wait when he calls you to come home?" Jason asked. "If you took life a little more seriously, you wouldn't be flunking out of school."

"Whatever, man," Ronnie said. "Ain't nobody flunking out..."

"Y'all chill," I said. "If Jason wants to read the Bible, more power to him."

"Anyway," Ronnie said, "what's up with you and Vanessa, Julian?"

"Nothing's up," I answered. "We're just friends."

"The hell with being just friends," Ronnie said. "She's fine, bro."

"She's not feeling me like that," I said. "She's sprung on that dude from I-State."

"Doing her calculus homework for her didn't score you any points, huh?" DeQuan asked.

"Nah, I'm afraid not," I answered.

"What's that dude's name?" Ronnie asked.

"His name is Bryce," I answered. "He's dogging her out, but she's too blind to see it."

"Yeah, I know him," Jason said. "He's got mad women up there."

"I saw him posted up with three women at a party up there three weeks ago," DeQuan added. "He's definitely living up to the Q-Dog name."

"What do you have going on this weekend, Jason?" I asked, changing the subject.

"Nothing much outside of studying for these finals," Jason answered. "I got church on Sunday, of course."

"What made you do this complete one-eighty," I asked. "No offense, but you've done enough partying for all of us."

"None taken," Jason said, "and you're right. I had a vision that completely changed my life."

"What kind of vision?" DeQuan asked.

"God showed me that if I didn't stop binge drinking and experimenting with drugs, I'd be dead in five years. After that, I decided to become a born-again Christian."

"What does that mean?" Ronnie asked. "Born again? You can only be born once, homeboy."

"Not in the literal sense, Ronnie," Jason answered. "God says you are born again spiritually when you ask for forgiveness with a pure heart and accept Jesus as your Lord and Savior, and all of your sins will be forgotten."

"Just like that?" Ronnie asked.

"Yep, just like that," Jason answered.

"Even if you murdered somebody, God will forgive you?" Ronnie asked.

"Yes, it doesn't matter who you are or what you've done," Jason answered. "If you truly ask for forgiveness, you will be saved."

"Man, that's B.S.," Ronnie said. "You make it sound like a free-for-all or a sale at Target or something."

"Forgiveness *is* free, Ronnie," I said. "You'd be surprised how many people don't realize that."

"What else did God show you in the vision?" DeQuan asked curiously.

"God showed me when my true birth date was," Jason answered.

"Huh?" I asked, giving Jason my full attention. "Your true birth date?"

"Yes, my true birth date, not when man says we are born," Jason answered.

"How did he show you?" I asked.

"Not long after I recommitted myself to church, God sent me a birthday card in a dream I had three days before my actual birthday," Jason answered. "He told me that I have unique gifts and talents."

"Maybe he just wanted you to have it three days early," Ronnie added.

"Nah, man, you don't get it," Jason said. "When does a baby truly finish developing? No one really knows because man says life starts once you exit the womb, but to me, life starts inside the womb because you are breathing your mother's air and eating her food."

"That sounds crazy, Jason," Ronnie said.

"Nah, Ronnie, Jason went deep with this one," I said. "I guess I never thought of childbirth like that. You can be finished developing days before you exit your mother's womb...maybe even a week."

"Right, now you see where I'm coming from, Julian," Jason said.

I remembered that conversation like it was yesterday. Ronnie Clark dropped out of school after two years and became a bus driver for the Chicago Transit Authority, and I never saw Jason Harris again after graduation. I often wondered what became of Jason—I could definitely see him being a pastor of a church because he was so into the word of God.

Out of the blue, Vanessa's *beau*, Batavia, walked in moments after I gulped the last of my drink. She was carrying a gym bag and walked to the back of the club where the other girls congregated. This was turning out to be a very interesting night.

11

I thought of leaving the club because I really wasn't feeling it, but I ended up staying instead. There were too many guys present for my taste, and I wasn't the type of guy who threw money around at some strip joint. However, if I hadn't decided to stay, I wouldn't have seen Batavia. I pictured her as a young woman who worked a nine-to-five—perhaps a teacher like Vanessa—but I never would have guessed in a million years that she was a stripper.

There was a harem of women standing near the room with the pool tables and dartboard, and this tall drink of water captured my full attention. She was a chocolate beauty with probably the longest legs I have ever seen on a woman, and she wasn't wearing any panties. It amazed me how comfortable she was in a room full of guys half-naked.

She raised her miniskirt up to her crotch so that she could give all of us a sample of how perfectly shaped her butt was, and then she sat on the lap of a guy who pulled out a wad of cash. It must have been at least a couple thousand in his money clip from what I could see. I couldn't, nor was I trying to, compete with guys who had money to burn like that. Even when I was doing well, I never thought of flashing my cash like some high-rolling drug dealer.

I decided to lay in the cut with my beer and observe the whole scene. I was definitely out of touch with what was going on, but I didn't judge. It was easy money for a girl trying to make a come-up, and with the economy being the way it was, I was surprised that more women weren't doing it. The days of me using morality in my decision-making process were long gone, and besides, doing the right thing for most of my life didn't change my son's fate.

I had zoned out as I became entranced in the music—I think the DJ was mixing the song *Tap Out*, the stripper's anthem, when someone tapped me on the shoulder. That someone turned out to be Batavia.

"What are you doing here, Julian?" she asked.

I opened my mouth, but no words came out. She was wearing a see-through black teddy and black, six-inch stilettos, and she smelled so damn good. She was slightly taller than I was in her heels, and that turned me on.

"Julian?" she asked as her beautiful smile widened. "Don't you hear me talking to you?"

"I'm sorry, Batavia," I answered. "You caught me off-guard."

"You still didn't answer my question, baby."

"I heard the Cozy Inn was the spot that's poppin', so I decided to check it out for myself. So, how long have you been dancing here?"

"About a couple of months."

She then paused and said, "Come with me."

"Where?"

"Just come on."

"Okay, lead the way."

She led me to one of the dimly lit rooms that had a couple of leather sofas, a stocked mini-bar, and mirrors on every wall. *Pull Up to the Bumper* by Grace Jones was playing, and for the first time in my life, I actually paid attention to the lyrics of the song.

Pull up to my bumper, baby. In your long black limousine. Pull up to my bumper, baby. And drive it in between...

I was a little kid when the song came out—maybe seven or eight years old—and in my naivety at the time, I thought Grace Jones was actually singing about driving. I had no idea that song was about sex until that very moment.

Batavia took my hand and steered me to one of the sofas after she shut the door. She then removed the straps of her teddy, and it fell to her feet on the floor. I sat down on the sofa and stretched out my arms.

I pulled out a twenty-dollar bill, and she said, "Your money is no good here. Put that away."

I did what I was told and put the folded twenty back in my pocket. She sat on my lap completely naked and started grinding with her back facing me. I remained calm and abided by house rules, keeping my hands off of the girl. To my surprise, she placed both of my hands on her supple breasts as her slow grind turned into a full-blown dry hump.

I got caught up in the moment and started kissing on her neck and earlobe while massaging her bosom. She turned around to face me, she put her arms around my neck, and I placed my hands on her smoothly waxed thighs. Her legs were the perfect combination of soft and toned as they glistened in the subtle light. We then kissed passionately for several minutes before she pulled away. She then unzipped my pants to my surprise and pulled out a condom.

"I can't do this," I said abruptly. "You're my ex-wife's girl."

"I'm sorry," she said. "I thought you'd be game for it."

"No, I'm not game for this. I've known Vanessa over half of my life, and she definitely wouldn't understand us going behind her back."

"I guess you know her better than I do."

"That was the reason we got together in the first place—she found out her ex was sleeping with another girl and didn't tell her about it while we were in college. I, for one, am not gonna make that same mistake."

She got off of my lap and put her scanty undergarment back on. I remained seated until my excitement wore off.

"You're a great guy, Julian," she said. "Most guys would've taken me up on my offer anyway."

"Thank you, Batavia," I said. "You're a beautiful woman, but I can't betray Vanessa like that. This whole situation is a little weird to me."

"I understand," she said abruptly. "You're welcome to have a beer in the fridge—I have to get back to work. Take care of yourself, Julian."

"Thanks, I will."

She shut the door behind her after leaving the room. I tried to wrap my mind around what had just taken place. This was Vanessa's girl, who didn't know me from Adam and who wanted to have sex with me in a public place. I knew that it had to be a test, and I fought with every ounce of strength I had not to get caught up.

I then made my way back to the main entrance of the club, and I saw Batavia giving another guy a lap dance as if what we had just done never took place. Seeing her resume to business as usual didn't bother me at all, and my lack of concern let me know that I didn't get immersed in my attraction to her by overanalyzing the situation.

I left the club, and the once empty lot was now full of cars. I had the day off, and my plan was to go home and sleep off my intoxication. Once I found my car, I sat in the lot for a few more minutes to sober up somewhat.

My eyes weren't wide shut for the first time in my life—people, in general, tend to see the world the way they want to see it, not the way it really is. I lived my life that way for almost forty years, but now, I felt as though my head wasn't in the sand anymore.

12

Working six days a week kept my mind off Miles and helped with the healing process. It was July 6th—my birthday—and I was hard at work assisting customers and managing the floor at the store. The store manager was off that day, and it was mad busy.

The salary wasn't even close to what I made as an accountant, but it paid the bills. I made almost six figures before I was let go, and the idea of making a fraction of what I used to make sickened my stomach at times. I chose to go in another direction because my pride wouldn't let me take a step backwards in my field.

I was about to take a fifteen-minute break when a guy walked in with his son. The boy was about Miles's age, and it took all the strength I had not to lose it in the front of the customers. The man asked me where he could find some lawn bags, and I directed him toward aisle three. I quickly went to the break room afterwards, and luckily, no one was in there. It was then I broke down momentarily before regaining my composure. I had thought I was finished grieving for Miles, but I never knew what would trigger a flood of emotions at any given time. I guess I still had a soul after all.

It felt strange working on my birthday because I always reserved that day for Vanessa when we were married, but it had been Miles and me for the last couple of years. I just wasn't up for celebrating it without him. I didn't even get a call or text from Vanessa wishing me a happy birthday, either.

The crowd finally died down at about seven, and I was a few minutes from clocking out. Vanessa had shown up right before my shift ended, and I was pleasantly surprised. She was as stunning as ever, and her hair looked like she just left the beauty salon. She also wore an outfit that made my jaw drop to the floor—a black mini dress that fit her body like a glove and boots that came right above her knees.

"I like your hair," I said, "and you look absolutely amazing in your outfit."

"Thank you, Julian," she said. "You don't look too bad yourself."

"Thank you. So, what brings you by?"

"Your birthday. Let me take you out to dinner somewhere...my treat."

"I was beginning to think that you forgot about me."

"I wanted to surprise you and to apologize for the way I behaved at Jake's party. I didn't mean to catch you off-guard."

"All is forgiven. Your lifestyle is your business, Vanessa. Who am I to judge?"

"Yeah, but I didn't mean to rub it in your face like that. We had a little too much to drink before coming to the party."

"Drunk people tell no lies..."

"Indeed, they don't."

There was a brief pause, and I said, "Give me a few minutes to finish up here, and I'm all yours."

"Okay, I'll be waiting outside in the lot."

She smiled and winked at me before she exited the store, and I finished my list of daily duties before I left. The other assistant manager was closing up shop, so I didn't have any end-of-day processing to do. I spotted Vanessa's sparkling red BMW easily out of the myriad of parked cars in the lot.

"You don't ever worry about getting car-jacked in this ride?" I asked as I hopped inside her car. "I was worried the first day that you showed it off to me."

"I can't live my life in fear," she answered.

"I know. So, where are we going?"

"It's a surprise...you'll see."

We left the store lot and headed in the direction of the Dan Ryan Expressway. We were downtown in no time, and she drove us to the

River North area of the Loop. She pulled up in front of the Weber Grill restaurant and valeted the car.

"I've never been here before," I said.

"The food is great," she said. "I'm sure you'll love it."

We went inside, and she had reserved a table for us. It was typically crowded for a Saturday evening, and the server brought us our drinks right away. She ordered sangria, and I had a Miller Draft.

"So, what have you been up to these days?" she asked.

"I've been super busy at the store," I answered.

"I'm so happy for you, Julian...I know how hard it's been to find a job."

"It's been a long time coming, and it's paying the bills. Tomorrow is my first day off in ten days."

"That has to be against the law working that many days in a row," she said.

"I'm just getting back on my feet, and I need the money anyway," I said. "Being out of work for a while kind of changes your perspective on things."

"I totally understand, sweetheart."

I paused and said, "I saw Batavia at the Cozy Inn a few weeks ago."

"Oh yeah?" she asked. "That's where I met her, too."

"A stripper—I totally wasn't expecting to see her there. I thought she was a teacher like you."

"No, she's definitely not a teacher. I don't think I'd feel comfortable with somebody like her teaching our son."

"Somebody like her?"

"Come on, Julian, I know you're not blind. In case you didn't notice, Batavia is a ho. She wanted to sleep with me in one of the private rooms at the club after a free lap dance and make-out session. That night at Jake's party was our first and last date."

"So, your relationship with her wasn't too serious, huh?"

"No, I wasn't feelin' her like that, and I'm not feelin' being single anymore, either. The whole dating scene has drastically changed."

"I couldn't tell that you weren't into her...you two seemed pretty cozy to me."

"Things aren't always what they seem."

"Well, she gave me a free lap dance, too, and she wanted to have sex with me in one of the private rooms as well. I guess that's her m.o."

"Really?"

"Yeah, I'm afraid so."

"Damn, I'm glad that you told me."

"I'd never stab you in the back, Vanessa."

The waitress brought our food—Vanessa ordered a steak, and I had the grilled meatloaf. The food smelled good and tasted even better. We also ordered several more rounds of drinks, and we ran up a nice tab. An hour and a half had passed, and I was fully stuffed with a nice buzz going on. The waitress then asked us if we needed anything else, and Vanessa told her to bring the bill.

"You should let me give you something on that," I said.

"Don't be silly," she said. "It's your birthday. I got it."

"Well, in that case, thank you for a lovely dinner."

"You're very welcome, Julian."

She reached for her purse, and I noticed her perfectly manicured, French-tip nails. At that moment, I realized she got all jazzed up just for me.

She paid the server, and we left. She then brought me back to the store where my car was parked, and the lot was fairly empty. It was a 24-hour spot, and there were peaks and valleys of customer traffic throughout the course of any given night.

"I had a great time," I said.

"So did I," she said.

"I really don't want the night to end yet, but I think I should go home."

"Me neither. A friend of mine from work is throwing a party on the north side..."

"I really don't do parties anymore; Jake's party was the exception. I'd be content with just going to a lounge and having a drink but not tonight."

"That's fine. Suit yourself. Don't be a stranger, okay?"

"Okay."

She leaned into me for a brief kiss, and her soft, cherry-lip-gloss-coated lips tasted so sweet. I was in the process of mentally talking myself out of taking things any further but to no avail. Vanessa's kisses always had a way of disarming me.

"I really miss you, Julian," she said.

"I really miss you, too," I said.

"We can help each other get through the pain that I know we're both feeling, Julian. I love you."

"I love you, too, but love isn't enough."

"What if I told you that I wanted to be married to you again?"

"I want to believe you, Lord knows I do, but you can't just turn me on and off like a light switch."

"I know but being single hasn't brought me any long-term happiness or satisfaction, and I destroyed our marriage because I thought I was missing out on something in this wacked dating scene. Call it a middle-life crisis."

"I thought men only experienced that."

"No, sometimes, women go through the same kind of changes. We're just not as overt as men are—usually."

"What if you have the urge to be with another woman again?"

"I won't—because I'm not a lesbian or bisexual—and like I said before, I haven't experimented with any women since college. I thought the grass was greener on the other side, but now, I realize what I lost with you."

"Have you been with any men?"

"No..."

"Really?"

"No, I haven't—just a few dates, but nothing more than that. Have you been with any women?"

"Yes, one."

"Who?"

"Why does it matter?"

"Who, Julian?"

I sighed and said, "Brandy Stewart from the office. We hooked up after having a few drinks after work, and one thing led to another. She was ready to leave her husband for me, but I ended our brief affair because I couldn't be the one who broke up their family."

"Wow, how noble of you, Julian," she said sarcastically. "I always knew that she had a thing for you."

"What did you expect, Vanessa? I was heartbroken after we split up..."

"I know you were, and I'm sorry you had to go through that."

Vanessa paused momentarily and said, "I don't know what the future holds, but I do know that I want us to be together again."

"Are you seeing anyone right now?"

"I told you I wasn't..."

I grabbed her arm and pulled her toward me before we locked lips with each other. Our kiss was long and passionate as we tightly embraced each other for what seemed like an eternity. I eventually let go of my embrace and stepped back from her as a way of combating the urge to strip her naked in the parking lot.

"I need to take things slowly with you, Vanessa. I'm not saying no, but I'm not saying a definite yes, either. I can't afford to invest another twenty years into a lie."

"That's fair, Julian. I can't ask for any more than that."

"Call me and let me know that you got home safely."

"I will, baby. I love you."

"I love you, too," I said, kissing her lips once more for a brief moment.

She got in her car, and I watched her taillights fade in the distance. Part of me wanted to dive right into a relationship with Vanessa because I missed her so much, but I had the strength to push the pause button. My mind had overridden my heart—this time. Finally, I left the parking lot after ten minutes or so and went home.

13

I had softened my stance on finding Miles's killer for the time being and focused on work and paying my bills. Vanessa and I would occasionally spend time with each other—a day off for me was few and far between because I didn't have a set schedule like she did.

It was a blazing hot Friday morning, and I was on my way to the barbershop to get a haircut and shave. My appointment was at ten, and I was my barber, Jessie's, first customer. It had been months since I'd been back to the shop—Miles and I used to go see Jessie every week together without fail after Vanessa moved out to Riverdale over two years ago after we sold our condo in Bronzeville. His shop was only a mile away in the neighboring suburb, Dolton. I had been doing my own grooming but decided it was okay for me to assimilate into the general population again.

"Julian, what's the good word, my man?" Jessie asked.

"I can't complain, Jessie," I answered.

"Hey, man, I heard about Miles...sorry."

"It's all right...I'm just taking it day by day. Things are getting a little easier as time moves on."

"That's great to hear, and I'm glad to have you back."

"I'm glad to be back."

"Well, let's get you trimmed up, so you can go on about your day."

And that's exactly what Jessie did—he promptly sat me in his chair and went to work on making me look presentable. Two more patrons entered the shop right after I began to get touched up. They both looked like young thugs in training and were loud and obnoxious.

"Yo, man, that chick was thick," thug number one said. "You were throwin' bills at her like you tryin' to cop her or sumthin'."

"Yeah," thug number two said, "that was the plan, bro."

"Hey, fellas," Jessie said. "Binky and Wes will be here in a minute to take care of y'all."

"Aiight, Jessie," thug number one said. "Thanks."

They continued talking but lowered their voices an octave. I could still hear their conversation clearly without trying to listen to it.

"When does ol' boy wanna see us?" thug number two asked.

"We're gonna holla at him tonight at the spot," thug number one answered.

"The Cozy?"

"Yeah, he wants to go over the plan with us there."

"How much are we gettin' paid?"

"Five up front and five when it's done."

"Cool."

Thug number two paused and said, "Your boy messed up, and he's gonna get taxed."

"Yeah, what went down in Ivanhoe Park that day was bad for biz," thug number one said.

I perked up when I heard Ivanhoe Park. What went down? Were they talking about Miles's shooting? My heart began to race, and I fought fiercely to remain calm. They were talking in semi-code, and I deciphered that they were probably talking about performing a hit on somebody. I couldn't believe they were so bold about it and wondered if Jessie picked up on their conversation. They had quickly changed the subject and started talking about a dice game they had lost money on.

Jessie put the finishing touches on my hair and beard, and I tipped him a few minutes later. He handed me the mirror to look at myself, and I smiled back at myself in approval.

"You never disappoint me," I said. "I promise I won't stay away again."

"I'mma hold you to that, Julian," he said. "See you next week."

"You bet, Jessie. Take care."

I kept my cool and left the shop. I didn't believe in fate until that very moment—I was being tested and knew I was going to flunk with flying colors. Curiosity was going to lead me to the Cozy Inn, and nothing was going to stop me from getting to the truth. Maybe I was wrong—maybe a hit wasn't going down like I thought I heard. I had two options—walk away and completely wash my hands of the whole sordid mess or get to the bottom of what happened to my son. The former wasn't an option for me, and somehow, I had to find the right words to say to Vanessa about what I was planning on doing that night. Dating Vanessa again was exactly what the doctor ordered, and I wasn't trying to lose her. However, I was prepared to go the distance, even if it meant killing everyone involved.

14

I called Vanessa and asked her to meet me at my house after she got off work. It was Friday, and ordinarily, she was done teaching by two thirty unless she had a parent-teacher conference or something to that effect. I didn't know what I was going to say to her about what I had learned, and I certainly didn't know how she was going to react. I felt like I owed her the truth, so she could make a decision on whether or not to continue dating me. Either way, the person or persons responsible for Miles's death were going to pay, even if it meant losing her in my life.

I had finished running my errands for the afternoon on my day off and got home a little before three thirty. Vanessa was already parked in front of my house when I arrived, and we embraced and kissed each other on my front lawn after I parked my car.

"I missed you," she said.

"I missed you, too," I said as we both stepped inside my house.

"So, what did you want to talk about?" she asked.

"I think I know who killed our son," I answered.

"Really? Who?"

"I was at the barbershop this morning and overheard a conversation between two dudes while I was getting a haircut. They were talking in code, and I believe they're getting paid to kill the guy responsible for shooting Miles."

"Why do you think that they were talking about the guy who killed Miles?"

"Because one of the guys said that they were going to tax this guy for bringing too much heat to their business in Ivanhoe Park."

"I see. So, what are you going to do about it?"

"I'm going to find out who's responsible and make him pay...I just wanted to give you the heads-up before I carry out my plan."

"What plan, Julian? Why don't you just tell the police?"

"I don't feel comfortable going to the police, Vanessa..."

"Well, I have a problem with you trying to be a damn detective. You can tell Jake what you overheard at the barbershop."

"I can't..."

"Why the hell not?"

"Because I killed three people in the alley behind my house a week before Jake's birthday party..."

"You did what? Are you crazy, Julian?"

"No, Vanessa, it was self-defense."

"When did you get a gun?"

"I bought a .380 semi-automatic after my neighbor Melvin got carjacked last year, and I bought another one after Miles got killed."

"So, how did it happen?" she asked as her eyes began to get watery.

I gave her the entire spill from the time I arrived at the bar to the confrontation in the alley. Tears streamed down her face as I finished telling her the story. She grabbed my hand and said as she wept, "I don't want to lose you, Julian. The police are eventually going to find out what happened."

"I don't think that girl is going to snitch," I said, "or else she would've done it by now. She doesn't even know who I am."

"These things always have a way of coming out, and it's still illegal to carry a gun in Illinois."

"Quan destroyed the guns, so the police can't directly link me to the murder. Any evidence against me would be purely circumstantial."

"Who are you? An expert?"

"Why are you riding me? If I wasn't strapped that night, I'd be dead."

There was dead silence for a moment. Vanessa got up from the sofa and went to the kitchen to get a paper towel. She wiped the tears off her face and blew her nose before washing her hands in the sink. She then got two beers from the fridge and handed me one.

"You have to tell Jake what happened," she said as she sat back down on the sofa.

"I can't tell him what happened because he *is* the police," I said, taking a sip of my beer.

"Jake's your brother first—and he'd know what to do. Besides, you can't take on those guys by yourself."

I picked up my cell phone from the living room table and called Jake. He picked up on the third ring.

"What's up, bro?" he asked.

"Are you working today?" I asked.

"Yeah, my shift is over in about an hour," he answered. "Why?"

"Can you swing by my house? I need to share something very important with you as soon as possible."

"Okay, give me about an hour, and I'll be there."

"Alright, see you then."

I disconnected the call and turned to face Vanessa.

"He'll be here in about an hour," I said.

"Thanks for listening to me," she said. "Everything will work out for the better—you'll see."

"I hope so."

She grabbed my hand again and began caressing it. Her presence calmed my spirit, and she laid her head on my shoulder before I put my arm around her. I didn't want to go to jail for the rest of my natural life, and Vanessa helped me to see that my actions were going to lead me down that path to destruction. Before we knew it, we fell asleep in each other's arms.

15

The sound of my doorbell broke our slumber and startled both of us as I slowly rose from the sofa to answer the door. I noticed that twilight had set in, and I unlocked the door and found Jake standing in front of it. He apologized before I could let him in.

"I know I was supposed to be here hours ago," Jake said, "but I got caught up in some business at the precinct."

"Don't sweat it," I said after I yawned. "What time is it?"

"It's little after eight," Jake answered. "Hey, sis."

"Hey, Jake," Vanessa said.

"You all back together?" Jake asked.

"We're working on it," Vanessa answered.

"Yeah, we're taking things slowly," I added.

"That's great," Jake said. "We've all missed you, Vanessa."

"That's nice to know," Vanessa said, "and I've missed you guys as well."

"So, bro, what's so urgent that you wanted to talk about?" Jake asked.

I evaded Jake's question initially. How do you tell someone who happens to be your brother and who happens to be a member of the Fraternal Order of Police that you killed three people in self-defense? I went to the kitchen to grab three beers from the fridge instead, and I handed one of them to him before sitting on the sofa next to Vanessa.

"Thanks," Jake said. "You didn't answer my question, Julian."

I paused for a second before twisting the cap off my Miller Draft and asked, "Remember when you tried to call me that weekend I was back home in St. Louis?"

"Yes, I remember," Jake answered. "You didn't hit me back until the day you came back to Chicago."

I got up from the sofa and began to saunter around the living room with beer in hand before saying, "I left Chicago because of that triple homicide in the alley behind my block..."

"Did you see something that night?" Jake asked curiously.

"Yeah, you could say that," I answered, still searching for the right words to convey to him.

"What, Julian?" Jake asked.

"I, uh, was the one who shot those three guys in the alley," I answered.

"What?" Jake asked. "Have you lost your damn mind, Julian?"

"That's exactly what I asked him," Vanessa added.

"It was self-defense, Jake," I answered.

"Why didn't you tell me?" Jake asked. "You could've just told me, man."

"Because you're the damn police," I answered, "and telling you what happened obligates you to turn me in."

"I'm not going to turn you in," Jake said. "I'm still your brother above everything else."

"I told him that too," Vanessa interjected.

"How did this happen?" Jake asked.

I told Jake the sordid details of that fateful night, and he listened intently. I had finished my beer before finishing the story.

"Where are the guns?" Jake asked.

"Quan dismantled them," I answered.

"So, he knows about what happened?" Jake asked.

"Yep," I answered.

"And that girl set you up?" he asked.

"Yes, she did," I answered.

"She told the police that they were ambushed in the alley by a rival gang," Jake said.

"She admitted that her boyfriend was in a gang?" I asked.

She said the guy had left the gang and was trying to get his life together," he answered. "She made it seem like they were innocent victims."

"Innocent victims, huh?" I asked rhetorically. "Nothing about them says innocent, and if a gang would've ambushed them, she'd be dead, too."

"I thought the same thing, but she stuck with her story after eight hours of questioning," he said.

"She lied because she feared going to jail," I said.

"Yeah, most likely," Jake said. "She has no living witnesses other than you to collaborate or counter her story. Saying a gang did it clears her of any wrongdoing."

Jake paused for a moment and said, "Even though the shooting in the alley was self-defense and witnesses can possibly verify the confrontation at the bar, it's still illegal to carry a firearm in Illinois. However, the law might change next year."

"Can Julian go to jail?" Vanessa asked.

"Yeah, for a minimum of three years, I'm afraid," Jake answered.

"So, what's the next move?" I asked.

"I don't know," Jake replied. "I need a little time to think."

"Julian knows who might've killed our son," Vanessa said. "That's the other reason he called you."

"Yeah, who?" Jake asked.

"I overheard two guys at the barbershop talking about doing a hit," I answered. "They also mentioned that something bad for business happened in Ivanhoe Park."

"That's too much of a coincidence," Jake said. "When are they going to carry out the hit?"

"They said something about meeting up at the Cozy Inn tonight," I answered.

"Alright, we're in there," Jake said. "Let's go."

"Whose car are we taking?" Vanessa asked. "Not mine, I hope."

"We can take mine," Jake said. "I'm not a cop tonight, you all. Miles was like a son to me, and these punks are going to pay."

16

All eyes were on Vanessa when the three of us entered the club. She was undoubtedly a natural-born trendsetter with her ensemble of clothes and jewelry—and she could've easily been the lead character in the movie *The Joneses,* instead of Demi Moore. We walked toward the bar, and I could feel the stares like laser beams lighting us up. I was used to it though—my life had changed forever when Vanessa and I hooked up on Bradley University's campus some twenty years ago. I was basically a nobody until she chose me. Afterwards, every fraternity on the yard knew my name and wanted me to pledge, and a few women even tried to get me to veer in another direction when Vanessa wasn't looking. Most of the guys wondered how I managed to pull the finest girl on campus, and I would simply say persistence always pays off.

We sat down at the bar and ordered our drinks as Vanessa checked her makeup with the camera on her cell phone, and Jake and I observed the whole scene—a few guys were typically hanging on the walls gawking at all the women that passed by, another guy was bragging about what he had done to some unsuspecting woman who lent him her ear to pass time, and the rest of them didn't have a damn clue as to what was going on.

"Do you see them yet?" Vanessa asked.

"Not yet," I answered before taking a swig of my beer.

"Let me know when you do, so I can get the ball rolling," Jake said.

"What you got planned?" I asked.

"I'm gonna flash my badge, ask them a few questions," he answered.

"You're not a cop tonight, remember?" I asked. "Let me quarterback this thing and you back me up."

"No, Julian," Vanessa interjected. "Let Jake handle this."

"I was there, and I remember every detail just like it was yesterday," I said. "I'm not walking out of here until I find out the truth, so help me God."

"Okay, but I'm still taking the lead just in case these fools try to pop off," Jake said.

"Whatever," I said.

We continued to sit at the bar and wait. We ran up a nice tap for another hour or so before the guys that I saw at the barbershop walked in. It was like they parted the Red Sea as they made their way to a table on the right side of the bar. A barmaid brought them a bottle of Patron and two glasses.

"That's them," I said.

"Where, over there?" Jake asked, pointing to the right of us.

"Yeah, those two clowns," I answered.

"Let's make it happen," Jake said.

"Not yet," I urged. "They're supposed to be meeting the guy who's giving them the cash for the hit, so let's wait until the third guy shows up."

"That sounds like a plan, little brother," Jake said. "You sure you don't wanna be a cop?"

"No," Vanessa and I said in unison.

Moments later, my college buddy Ronnie walked up to our table. He had on a wife-beater and baggy jeans, and he was all tatted up with his drink in hand. Ronnie was the only guy from our college clique I'd run into periodically—I had yet to see Jason.

"What's up, Ronnie?" I asked as I stood up from our table to give him a hug.

"I'm living, bro," Ronnie answered. "Taking it one day at a time."

"You all remember Ronnie?" I asked.

"Of course I do," Vanessa answered, giving him a hug. "It's great seeing you."

"Thanks, you too," Ronnie said.

"You look good, old man," Jake said, shaking his hand before giving him a hug. "Nice to see you again."

"Likewise, big bro," Ronnie said. "Sorry about Miles, guys...I had to work on the day of the funeral."

"It's okay, Ronnie," I said. "We're dealing with it the best way that we can."

"Hey, if you all need anything, I'm here for you," Ronnie said.

"Thanks," I said. "So, what have you been up to?"

"I'm still with the CTA," Ronnie answered. "Five more years, and I'm at twenty-five. I'm retiring after that."

"I hear you," Jake said. "Hell, driving a bus these days is dangerous, anyway."

"Not as dangerous as being a cop," Ronnie said.

"Touché," Jake said.

"On the real," Vanessa said, "somebody just got shot on the Ashland bus the other day."

"Yeah, you watch your back out here, Ronnie," I said.

"I always do, good people," Ronnie said.

I looked at his right biceps, and he had a tattoo of a baby boy on it.

"Is that your son on your arm?" I asked.

"Oh, yeah," Ronnie answered, "one of them."

"What's his name?" Vanessa asked.

"His name is Steven," Ronnie answered.

"How many kids you got?" Vanessa asked.

"Three, and two baby mamas," Ronnie answered. "Child support is wearing me out."

"Still a playa," Vanessa said.

"Yeah, I'm afraid so," Ronnie chuckled. "Old habits die hard."

"Yeah, and how in the hell are you going to retire with three kids?" I asked.

"I don't know, but I can't keep doing what I'm doing," Ronnie answered. "They're gonna force me out sooner or later anyway and offer me an early retirement package."

"You should take it," Jake said. "These institutions don't care about their employees anymore. I'll have twenty-five in five, too."

"What, you're thinking about retiring, Jake?" I asked.

"I don't know," Jake answered. "Maybe."

"No more talk about retirement," Vanessa said. "I have at least another ten years before I can even think about it."

"Well, I got laid off from my job six months after I saw you last, Ronnie," I said. "I had to reinvent myself, and now, I'm an assistant store manager."

"That's good," Ronnie said. "I know people who still can't find work after two years."

"What would you do with yourself once you retire, Ronnie?" I asked. "Forty-five is still young."

"I've got some money saved," Ronnie answered. "I've always wanted to open a restaurant—preferably a soul food restaurant."

"That's a great idea," I said. "You damn sure used to burn in college."

"Thanks, I've been thinking about it for a while," Ronnie said.

I paused briefly before saying, "We really should hang out, Ronnie—I mean it. These years are going by too fast."

"We will. I promise," Ronnie said. "The six of us can do a couple's night out."

"*You* got a girlfriend?" Vanessa asked.

"Yeah, Vanessa," Ronnie answered. "Is that so hard to believe?"

"Uh, yeah," Vanessa answered. "What's her name?"

"You'd like her, and her name is Aubrey," Ronnie answered.

"Aubrey?" Vanessa asked. "Is she Black?"

"Good seeing you, man," I said laughingly. "A couple's night out sounds good."

"Yeah, I'll be looking forward to it," Jake said.

He started to walk away before turning back around to face us.

"Hey Julian, I almost forget to tell you that I ran into Jason about two weeks ago," he said.

"Yeah?" I asked. "How's he doing?"

"He's doing exactly what we thought he'd be doing," he answered. "He pastors a church on the west side right off Cicero and Chicago Ave."

"That's good," I said. "Maybe I'll stop by there one day."

"Maybe I'll do the same," Ronnie said. "Well, see you all later."

We all said goodbye, and Ronnie disappeared into the crowd of people near the room with the pool tables and dartboard. Fifteen more minutes had passed before the third guy finally showed up. He sat down after shaking hands with the other two guys.

"The third guy just sat down at the table with the other two clowns," I said. "Let's go over there and say hello."

"Slow down, cowboy," Jake said. "This is going to require a little finesse."

"The hell with finesse," I said. "I'm going to mop the floor with the first punk that says something I don't like."

"Who do you think you are, Julian?" Vanessa asked. "These guys look like they are no joke..."

"Why are you treating me like I'm soft, Vanessa?" I asked angrily. "I'm not the least bit scared of these lowlife degenerates, and this *looking like no joke* thing goes both ways..."

"Calm down, Julian," Jake interjected. "We gonna go over there, I'm gonna flash my badge, and we're gonna asked them some questions, all right?"

"Whatever, man, let's just do it," I answered.

Jake and I got up from the table and walked toward the three young men. Vanessa sat and watched with a curious eye as Jake flashed his badge to them.

"That badge don't mean nothing to me," thug number one from the barbershop said. "Whatever it is that you come over here to ask us, the answer is *we don't know*."

"Strike one," I said.

"We didn't come over here to bust your balls," Jake said. "We just want to know if you know anything about a thirteen-year-old kid getting shot in Ivanhoe Park a few months ago..."

"I don't know nothing," thug number one said.

"What about you?" I asked, looking at thug number two from the barbershop. "You gonna let him speak for you?"

"I don't know nothing, either," thug number two answered. "What makes you think we know anything about some kid getting shot in Ivanhoe Park?"

"We can do this the easy way, or we can sort this all out at the station," Jake said.

"You have no probable cause to arrest us," the third guy interjected. "We don't have to tell you anything."

"Oh, we got a smart one here," I said. "That's strike two."

"Look, you can make this quick and painless by cooperating with us," Jake warned, "or I can call for backup right now and have the three of you *Mirandized* in eight minutes flat."

"Do what you gotta do," thug number one said. "I'm not saying a damn thing without my lawyer present."

"That's strike three," I said, "and lawyering up means you're guilty of something."

Jake reached in his pocket and pulled out his phone, but I grabbed his arm to stop him from placing the call.

"Don't phone it in yet," I said. "Look, man, I'm just gonna cut to the chase. I'll bet that one of you has five grand in his pocket right now—and—if I guess which one of you has bulging pockets, I get to keep the money."

"What the hell are you talking about?" thug number two asked.

"In case you haven't figured it out yet, I was at the barbershop this morning and overheard your conversation, stupid," I answered. "We're all here tonight because the three of you are conspiring to perform a hit, correct?"

I then looked directly at the third guy and said, "The five grand in your pocket is proof of conspiracy to commit murder and probable cause to arrest you. Tell us what you know about the murder in Ivanhoe Park, and all three of you can walk out of here free and clear—your choice."

The three of them looked at each other—undoubtedly pondering the offer that I'd given them. Finally, after about fifteen seconds or so of weighing their options, the third guy said, "The dude you're looking for name is Lametrius Wright—he was the one who shot that boy in the park that day."

"What does he look like?" I asked

"He's a short, dark-skinned dude," the third guy answered. "He also has an afro like that rapper Puffy first signed with Biggie."

"Craig Mac?" I asked.

"Yeah, him," the third guy answered.

"Where can we find him?" Jake asked.

"He stays in those apartments over on 140th and School Street in Riverdale, but he's probably at that bar on 138th and Indiana getting wasted right now," thug number one added.

"What's the name of the bar?" I asked.

"Jimmy's Place," thug number one answered.

"Alright, gentlemen, thank you for your time," Jake said. "Come on, bro, let's go."

I texted Vanessa and told her to meet us outside, and Jake and I waited by the car for her to come out. I put my phone back in my pocket and said, "That went a little smoother than I thought it would go. I guess they figured this cat wasn't worth going to jail for because they were going to kill him anyway."

"All jokes aside, Julian, you really handled yourself well in there," Jake said. "You already have in your arsenal what took me months to learn in the streets dealing with these criminals. You're a natural."

"I know where you're going with this, but the answer is still no," I said. "I'm doing this for Miles, and I won't rest until he gets justice."

"Okay, that's fair," Jake said.

Vanessa finally joined us in the lot outside the club. She turned to me and asked, "What's going on?"

"They told us who killed Miles," I answered.

"Who killed our son?" she asked.

"A guy named Lametrius Wright," Jake interjected. "I'm going to bring this guy in tonight."

"Don't you mean *we*?" I asked.

"No, I mean me—and Riverdale's finest backing me up," Jake answered. "You're going to take your wife home and let the police do their job."

"What happened to you not being a cop tonight?" I asked.

"Just let me do my job, Julian," Jake said. "I know you don't want this punk getting off on a technicality, and I promise that we will put him behind bars for a long time."

"Come on, baby," Vanessa said. "Let's take a cab back to your place. Jake can handle things from here."

"I'll call you the moment we have this guy in custody," Jake said.

"Okay, you win," I said reluctantly.

Vanessa called a cab to pick us up in the club's parking lot, and Jake left. A part of me was relieved that Miles's killer wasn't going to go unpunished, and all the anger I had bottled up inside was released once Jake had gone to apprehend the alleged suspect.

17

Our cab finally came after waiting forty-five minutes, and luckily for my pockets, Interstate 57 was only a couple of blocks from the club. We were both quiet for most of the ride before Vanessa broke the silence.

"Jake called me your wife," she said. "What do you think about that?"

"I haven't given it any thought because I didn't hear him call you my wife," I answered.

"Well, how do you feel about us being married again?"

"I think marriage is something that we need to discuss in the near future. I feel there's still a spark between us."

"There definitely a spark between us, but I still feel like you're holding back from me."

"I am...but I have to be sure I'm making the right decision."

"Well, do you feel like you're making the right decision?"

"Yes, but you have got to stop treating me like your child, Vanessa, or this relationship of ours isn't going to work."

"Child? When have I ever disrespected you, Julian? I have nothing but the upmost respect for you."

"No, I don't mean disrespectful...it's more like overprotective. You make me feel like I can't protect you as a man."

"I'm sorry...I don't mean to treat you like that. I'm just afraid of losing you like we lost Miles."

I paused for a second or two and said, "Remember when you woke up from being passed out in my bed after going to that Alpha party?"

"Yes, it was a few weeks before we became a couple, and you had slept on the couch in your living room. You told me that I had too much to drink and wouldn't let me go home by myself. You were the perfect gentleman."

"Yes, but that's only the half of it. Do you remember Mario Simmons?"

"Yes, he was an Alpha, right?"

"Right, and he had a huge crush on you—no—more like an obsession."

"Where are you going with this, Julian?"

"You weren't drunk, Vanessa. Mario tried to date rape you..."

"Date rape me?"

"Yes, he slipped a date-rape pill in your drink when you weren't looking, and you were in and out of consciousness before he tried to take you in his room at the Alpha house that night. I saw what he did and promptly beat him and one of his line brothers down."

"How come you never told me this?"

"Because I put Mario in the hospital, and he was going to press charges against me until I threatened to press charges against the entire Alpha chapter on your behalf. I'm sorry I never told you—I made a deal with the Devil because I didn't want to get expelled from school and possibly go to jail, and the Alphas didn't want to lose their chapter for Mario's attempted rape."

"How could you, Julian? How could you keep something like this from me all these years?"

"For the same reason that you didn't tell me about your sexual past. Look, neither one of us is perfect—you shared your dark secret, and I just shared mine. Let's just leave the past behind."

"How did you know he slipped that pill in my drink? Did you see him do it?"

"No, but I knew he had done it before. He had bragged to Ronnie once about how he slipped the pill in Rachel Barnes' drink and smashed her at one of their parties the previous semester. Ronnie told me the whole story afterwards."

"Why didn't Ronnie or you report him?"

"I don't know, baby—as young men, we adhere to the no-snitching code of conduct, I guess. However, I do know Ronnie stopped hanging out with him not long after that."

"Well, that explains why Mario never spoke to me after the party. He was probably afraid that I'd find out about what he did to me."

"And that's why I never pledged."

"You wanted to pledge Alpha?"

"At first, I did...before Mario tried to rape you."

There was brief silence again, and I could see Vanessa's mind churning before she said, "Thank you."

"You don't have to thank me, baby. The point I'm trying to make is I can handle myself out here, and I can protect you, too."

"I know you can, and I get it now. I promise I won't question your manhood ever again."

Vanessa leaned over and kissed me on the cheek. The cab driver double-parked in front of my house minutes later, and she pulled out her debit card and handed it to me. I examined the card and saw that her last name was still Brown.

"What are you doing?" I asked. "I've got cash in my pocket."

"You sure?"

"Here, take your card back."

I paid the driver and told him to keep the change, and we got out of the cab. The ride was a tad over a hundred dollars, so I gave him six twenties for enduring our taxicab confession. We walked hand-in-hand toward my porch before I planted a kiss on her cherry-flavored lips. We wasted no time striping each other down to our bare essentials in my living room, once I locked the door and led her to my bedroom, and we explored every inch of each other until it was practically sunrise. I guess one could say we undoubtedly missed each other.

Jake had texted me in the middle of our love-making session and informed me that Lametrius Wright was in custody at the Riverdale police station being questioned. A calmness that I hadn't experienced in quite some time came over me after I received his text.

"I love you, Julian," she whispered in my ear before pecking me on my cheek and laying her head back on my chest. "I promise never to let you go again."

"You are still my wife in my mind, even though we're divorced," I said. "I see you feel the same way because you didn't change your last name back to Stone."

"Yes, I do, and I felt regret the moment I filed those papers," she said. "I had to learn to live with my decision, though."

"Let's not dwell on the past, sweetheart. We can go to City Hall today and get married if you want."

"That's a good idea, but let's wait until the rest of the family can witness it. Maybe your friend Jason could marry us."

"Okay, it's settled. We can visit Jason's church on Sunday."

"Great."

"Jake texted me and said they have the guy in custody," I said, changing the subject.

"Really? That's the best news I've heard in months."

"My sentiment exactly."

"So, where do we go from here?"

"I guess we wait for the trial to begin."

"Hopefully, this case won't drag on."

"I pray that it doesn't."

We continued to snuggle in bed as the sun began to rise. We were fast asleep before we realized it.

18

Vanessa and I sat in the back pew on the right-hand side of the church and listened to Jason's powerful sermon Sunday afternoon. His message resonated in ways that my spirit never experienced in my forty years of existence. He talked about where our spirit goes when we die—that the realm we wake up in is based on how we lived here on Earth. If a person lived righteously, God and his angels would have an incorruptible, glorified body designed for the spirit world waiting for us. However, if a person lived unrighteously, there would be no body waiting for them and would be deemed unlawful to dwell in God's kingdom. The demons that ruled one's life would then have complete possession of their disembodied spirit and would drag one straight to Hell.

Jason style was bold and direct, and his message wasn't watered down or compromised in any way. We waited for the small crowd to dissipate before approaching Jason at the pulpit. He smiled once we made eye contact.

"How long has it been?" Jason asked as he gave both Vanessa and me a hug.

"Too long, man," I answered.

"Good to see you again," Vanessa said.

"You, too, Vanessa," Jason said. "Ronnie told you guys about me, huh?"

"Indeed, he did," I answered. "Your sermon was awesome, Jason. It's no surprise to us that you have your very own church."

"Thank you, Julian," Jason said. "Ronnie told me about your son— sorry, you all."

"Thanks, Jason," Vanessa said. "It hasn't been easy, but the pain isn't as intense as was initially."

"That's good to know," Jason said. "Ronnie also told me that you two are divorced."

"I see Ronnie told you a lot," I said, "and our divorce is one of the reasons we came to your church today."

"Really?" Jason asked. "I don't understand."

"What Julian is trying to say is that we want you to marry us," Vanessa interjected.

"You want me to marry you?" Jason asked.

"Yes," Vanessa answered. "Can you do that for us?"

"Of course I can," Jason answered. "I'm glad that you all worked things out."

"Yes, I am too," I said. "Our son's death made us realize that we can't live life without each other in it."

"When do you want to retie the knot?" Jason asked.

"Give us a few weeks, so we can accommodate the family," Vanessa said.

"Okay, keep me posted," Jason said.

We said our goodbyes and left the church. We had a long haul back to the south suburbs—I packed an overnight bag and spent the night at Vanessa's house Saturday night after going to the show and eating out afterward. We went to see the movie *Flight,* starring Denzel Washington, and ate dinner at Olive Garden. I had to work the middle shift starting early Saturday afternoon and ending at eight o'clock. Luckily, I had Sunday off to attend Jason's church.

I hopped on Interstate 290 going westward and merged onto Interstate 294 after passing through the suburbs of Oak Park, Maywood, and Hillside. Vanessa had a transponder on her windshield, so I didn't have to fumble around looking for quarters. I loved the way her BMW could pick up speed at the drop of a hat—driving her car for the first time had me hooked, and I wanted a luxury sports car of my own.

"I love the way this car handles the road," I said. "I'm trading in my car for something like this really soon."

"You should, baby," Vanessa said. "You only live once, and we work too hard not to treat ourselves to something nice every now and then."

"I totally agree. As soon as I save up a nice down payment, I am at the dealership."

"I'll give you money."

"You do have to do that. Once I sell my house and stack a little loot, I'll be okay."

"You want to sell your house?"

"Yeah, sweetheart—we can't continue to live in separate households once we're married again, and besides, you teach in the south suburbs. Moving back to the city would be an inconvenience to you."

"I totally disagree with you on this, Julian. Why can't I just move in with you?"

"You want to move into my house?"

"Yes, baby, I do. Living in Riverdale reminds me of what happened to Miles and being alone in that house has really been tough on me."

"The school board doesn't have the rule that states you have to live in the city where you teach?"

"That rule only applies to Chicago teachers."

"Say no more...you can move in with me as soon as you want. I have plenty of room."

"Yes, and that's my second point. You have a beautiful home...much nicer than my space. I can do wonders with the decor in that house."

"Do your magic, Vanessa. My home could use a little more warmth."

"What do you have going on for the rest of the day?" Vanessa asked, changing the subject.

"I just need to pick up some stuff for the house," I said. "I'll go to the new Walmart around my house."

"I have a date with the nail salon—I can come by your house once I'm done."

"Our house—welcome home."

"Thank you. I like the sound of that."

We arrived at Vanessa's house thirty minutes later, and I kissed her goodbye and left. We had eaten a big breakfast before going to church, so neither one of us was hungry yet. I was excited about starting a new life with Vanessa, and for the first time in a couple of years, I was looking forward to the future.

19

The parking lot was filled to capacity as the newly built shopping mall off of 83rd and the Dan Ryan was the new hot spot. There was also a Lowe's, a movie theater, and other various smaller venues in the area. Holland Road was the street that led directly to another slew of stores and restaurants a half-mile from the Walmart and Lowe's stores.

I took a parking space on the far end of the lot because it was the closest spot available. I'm not one to be driving around the lot for fifteen minutes trying to get space closest to the store. I then got out of my car, hit the alarm, and walked toward the store. The items that I needed consisted mostly of cleaning supplies, and I needed to buy some pre-electric shave for my face. Walmart was the only store that carried the brand I liked, Afta.

Suddenly, I was stopped dead in my tracks before I could get halfway to the store from my parked car. The girl from the nightclub was standing right in front of me when I looked up from reading Vanessa's text asking me to buy some Secret deodorant for her. We made eye contact with each other but said nothing at first. It was awkward to say the least—she had a look of solemnness that I can't fully explain. It was as if her dark brown, deep-set eyes could look through the window of my soul just like that night at the bar.

I finally broke the ice after our fifteen-second staring contest and said, "I'm Julian."

"Brianna," she said.

She was as beautiful as she was the night I saw her for the first time, but her aura was much different. She wasn't sporting the weave with the blonde streaks in it, and she was dressed rather conservatively with a blouse and loosely fitted slacks that hid her curvaceous frame. In fact, her Anita Baker type hairstyle made her look very classy.

"I'm truly sorry about what took place that night, Brianna," I said. "I hope you can forgive me someday for killing your boyfriend, but I had no choice."

"I know," she said, "and I have. That night changed my life forever."

"It changed mine forever, too."

"Do you know what it's like to experience the feelings of hate, remorse, sadness, and gratefulness simultaneously?"

"Yes, I do, believe it or not. My thirteen-year-old son was murdered three or so months before I crossed your path."

"Well, that's what I currently feel every day of my life, and I can't seem to turn off these feelings, Julian. I'm sorry for what I tried to do to you, and I regret the day I started robbing people with Cory and his crew. Please tell me how you deal with the pain of it all."

"One day at a time, and some days are tougher to deal with than others."

She took a deep breath and asked, "Why didn't you kill me?"

"Honestly, I don't really know," I answered. "I guess for the same reason you didn't have me killed or tell the police what really happened."

"Tell the police what really happened?"

"My brother was one of the cops assigned to your case—he told me you said it was gang related."

"Yeah, that's my story, and I'll stick to it to the bitter end if I have to—telling the police the real reason that we were all in the alley that night would've incriminated me—"

"Indeed, it would've."

"I'm not going to lie—for weeks I plotted your demise, but something inside of me wouldn't let me make that phone call. I was also thankful to be alive—thankful that you didn't turn your gun on me, even though I deserved it. My man is dead because of me..."

Brianna began to wail uncontrollably, and I instinctively put my arms around her in an attempt to comfort her. I never would have guessed in a million years that I'd be consoling the very woman who tried to kill me at the beginning of the summer.

"Let it go, Brianna," I said. "You have to just let it go."

I let go of my embrace, looked her in the eyes, and continued, "I've felt and still feel every emotion you're experiencing right now. You have to pray to God and leave your burden at the altar like I did this afternoon in church. That's the only thing that will set you free, Brianna."

"Just like that?" she asked.

"Yes, just like that."

She wrapped her arms around my waist and planted her head on my shoulder, and I hesitantly reciprocated by putting my arms around her again. She was in obvious pain, and I did my very best to calm her spirit. I held her for roughly another minute before she let go of her embrace. She kissed me on the cheek and said, "Thank you for letting me cry on your shoulder."

"You're welcome, Brianna," I said.

"I'm going to take your advice and try to leave my burden at the altar, but the church will probably burn down once I step foot in it."

"God can forgive anybody for anything—don't sell yourself short."

"Thanks, I won't."

"Take care of yourself, Brianna."

"Goodbye, Julian."

I watched her walk toward her black, Mercedes Benz M-Class SUV and wave at me as she drove off before waving back at her and walking in the direction of the store. I had a fleeting thought as to what she currently did to maintain her lifestyle and hoped that she turned away from her previous illegal activities, but I was more focused on getting the items that I needed as quickly as possible by the time I walked through the entrance because the lines were sometimes slow—especially on Sunday afternoons.

I had initially come to the conclusion that Brianna lived somewhere close in proximity, but I never saw her again after that afternoon. The good Lord knew we both needed some form of closure from the horrific night that altered our lives forever, and I took our brief encounter as such. I told Vanessa about what happened when she got home, and she felt that it was divine intervention as well.

20

It was a briskly cool autumn evening on Sunday, October 7th, and Vanessa and I had just gotten married for the second time at my house by Jason. We went through the process of taking photos, eating dinner, cutting the cake, and saying the toasts—all of the things that people typically do at weddings. We had a very small and cozy wedding that consisted of a total of fifteen people—my parents, Vanessa's parents, Vanessa's sister Geneva, Jake and Cindy, Ronnie and Aubrey, Jason and his wife Sarah, DeQuan, my business partner Samuel Taylor, and Vanessa and me.

The tide had finally turned in my favor, financially, when I decided to strike out on my own and start my own accounting firm with my 401K retirement money. I partnered with my old colleague and friend, Sam Taylor, to form Brown & Taylor, LLP. Prior to that, I was barely getting by working long hours as an assistant store manager and barely had enough time to do anything worthwhile with my life once I was able to come up for air. I learned my old accounting firm that let me go went up in smoke, and Sam and I were able to garner some of their clients before the rest were eventually swallowed up by other firms. We then hired some recent undergrads who just passed the CPA exam to assist us in getting our startup off the ground.

However, the murder trial of Miles's killer was an entirely different story. My faith in God was once again tested when Jake informed me a few weeks after the arrest that Lametrius Wright took a plea deal in exchange for his testimony against the rest of the members of the crew. He plead guilty to second-degree murder and received a fifteen-year sentence. The fact that he could potentially be out in seven and a half years angered and sickened me to my stomach for weeks on end until I left my burden at the altar once again. Maybe the good Lord had a plan for the young man's life or something to that effect.

I also learned that Vanessa was pregnant a few weeks before we got married, and I was certain she conceived the night we made love for the first time since we'd gotten back together. I was happy and scared at the same time—excited to be a father again but afraid of going through the pain of losing him or her if something were to happen again. Nevertheless, I blocked those negative thoughts out of my mind and basked in the moment.

My crew from college was all together for the first time since graduation, and it felt great. I was talking to my dad while everyone else was engaging in small talk, laughing and enjoying themselves.

"I'm proud of you, Son," my father said. "You worked things out with Vanessa and reclaimed your rightful place in her life."

"Thank you, Dad," I said. "I never stopped believing that we could get back together."

"I know I was tough on you and your brother, but I had to instill the right values in you all, so you could navigate properly in this world."

"I know, Dad—I didn't understand it growing up, but I understand it now."

"Well, go over there and enjoy the rest of the party with your friends. Your mother and I are going to hit the road."

"I appreciate you all coming on such short notice."

My mom gave me a hug and said, "Thanks for inviting us. The whole ceremony was beautiful, and the food was delicious."

"You can thank Cindy," I said. "She helped plan everything, and she cooked the food."

"You need to go into business for yourself, Cindy," my mom said. "Everything was wonderful."

"Thank you, Mom," Cindy said.

"I tell her that all the time," Jake chimed in, "but she doesn't want to quit the County."

"I don't blame you," my mom said. "You put in all of those years, so you might as well stay for your pension."

"I'll have enough years in five, but I won't have the age," Cindy said. "I'll decide then what I'm going to do."

My mom and dad said their goodbyes to everyone, and Jake wanted all of the guys to take a photo together. The women followed suit after we struck a few poses, and our guests began packing plates to go because most everyone had to work in the morning.

"I had a great time, and congratulations to you both," Jason said. "Don't be strangers, okay?"

"We won't," Vanessa answered, "and thanks again."

"No problem," Jason said.

"Nice meeting you all," Jason's wife, Sarah, said.

"Likewise," I said. "I'll be in touch, Jason."

"Later, brother," Jason said.

They said their goodbyes to everyone else, and DeQuan, Sam, Ronnie, and his girlfriend, Aubrey, said their goodbyes soon afterward. Vanessa's parents and Geneva finished packing their plates and bid us farewell, and Jake and Cindy were the only guests left. Cindy helped Vanessa put away the food and wash the dishes, and Jake and I small talked for a few minutes.

"Can you believe it?" I asked. "Vanessa and I back together again. It's gonna be forever this time."

"Yeah, you two belong together," Jake answered. "I'm happy for you both."

"Man, I've got so many plans for us."

"Like starting your own business—that took guts."

"It was fate—when I got that phone call from Sam, I had to act quickly. Everything else just fell in place after that."

"I'm sure you'll do well."

"Thanks, Jake. I'm sure we will."

I took a breath and asked, "Do you think Lametrius will get an early release from prison?"

"I don't know, Julian," Jake answered, "and nobody knows what the future holds. I was just as angry as you were when the prosecution accepted his plea deal. I was hoping he'd rot in jail for a very long time."

"What's done is done, Jake. I left it at the altar."

"Yeah, it's probably for the best."

Vanessa and Cindy finished cleaning up the kitchen and came back into the living room. Cindy had gotten their jackets from the bedroom.

"Thanks for everything, you guys," Vanessa said.

"That's what family's for," Jake said. "You were always my sister in spite of the divorce."

"Well, that dark chapter of our lives is behind us, right babe?" Vanessa asked me.

"Right," I answered, "and I appreciate you both for helping us."

"You're very welcome, brother-in-law," Cindy said.

"Well, I guess we're going to take off as well," Jake said. "I got Monday morning roll call."

"I totally understand," I said. "See you guys later."

Jake and Cindy grabbed their plates-to-go and left. Vanessa and I were finally alone and made ourselves cozy on my living room sofa, once we changed into our lounge wear. She laid her head on my shoulder and snuggled next to me. Her perfume and hair smelled so good.

"Welcome home, Mrs. Brown," I said.

"It's great to be home, Mr. Brown," she said.

"Where do you want to go? We've got at least a thousand dollars in gift money here."

"A cruise would be nice, but it's hurricane season."

"Right, and I'm not getting on anybody's cruise ship at this time of the year."

"What about Vegas? The weather out there is perfect, right now."

"I'm not really feelin' Vegas, babe—you know I'm not much of a gambler."

"There's more to do in Vegas besides gamble. They have comedy shows, concerts, and of course, shopping."

"Let me think about it for a moment..."

"Don't take all night, Julian. I have to book a flight somewhere before morning."

"You think we did the right thing by not telling the family about the baby?" I asked, changing the subject.

"Yeah, I think it's too soon," she answered. "Miles's death is still fresh on people's minds, I think."

"I don't know—I think the news of another baby is just what they need to hear. The family would celebrate us, no matter what."

"Okay, we can tell Jake and Cindy when we get back from wherever we're going."

"It was good seeing everybody again, wasn't it? You know, tonight was the first time the crew was all together since graduation."

"Yes, it was, and I was pleasantly surprised by Ronnie's girlfriend, Aubrey. She wasn't like the usual airheads he dates."

"Aubrey's nice. Hopefully, she's a keeper."

"What about your company?"

"Huh?"

"Are you going to be able to take some time off?"

"Oh, yeah, of course. Sam can handle things until I get back."

"Good, because we need this trip after everything that has happened. So, are we good for Las Vegas?"

"Yeah, go ahead and book our flights."

"Great, baby. I'm going to freshen up—wanna join me?"

"Absolutely, Mrs. Brown, I thought you'd never ask."

Made in the USA
Columbia, SC
05 September 2019